POTATOES ARE CHEAPER

By Max Shulman

Max Shulman

POTATOES
ARE
CHEAPER

1971

DOUBLEDAY & COMPANY, INC., GARDEN CITY, NEW YORK

All the characters in the book are fictitious,
and any resemblance to actual persons, living or dead,
is purely coincidental.

Library of Congress Catalog Card Number 70–139060
Copyright © 1971 by Max Shulman
All Rights Reserved
Printed in the United States of America
First Edition

FOR MY DEAR MARY

POTATOES ARE CHEAPER

Chapter One

Oh, sure, potatoes were cheaper all right, and so were tomatoes, just like Eddie Cantor kept singing on the radio, but who the hell had money to buy any except maybe Eddie Cantor?

But finally, thank God, we got a break. On March the 14th, 1936, Pa went down to the St. Paul public library just like he did every day as usual. Not that he was such a great reader; in fact he could hardly read at all, not English anyhow, except maybe for eviction and foreclosure notices. He could read Yiddish all right, but that didn't help because there were no Yiddish books in the St. Paul public library. But Pa went every day anyhow. What else could he do? He didn't have a job to go to, and if he stayed home Ma would give him the whammy all day long. So where else could he find that was (a) warm; and (b) free?

So on this March the 14th, 1936, we're talking about, Pa started walking into the library as usual, but he never got inside because he slipped on an icy step and fractured his tailbone. Or as my mother told the whole neighborhood, "He fell and broke his ass, my smart husband."

Naturally we sued the city. My cousin Herbie who

got out of law school five years ago took the case—his first case, as it happened. But he was confident. "Don't worry, Aunt Pearl," he told my mother. "We got 'em dead to rights. You'll collect fifty thousand minimum."

Herbie figured a little high. The actual settlement came to $125 of which the doctor grabbed twenty. Still and all, it was the biggest chunk of money we'd seen since my father took up unemployment back in 1929, and we had a family conference at five o'clock one evening to decide what to do with it.

The reason the conference was at five o'clock was that nobody talks in my house after 6 P.M. That's radio time. You never met a radio nut like my mother. I'll tell you how far it goes. Not only does she stay glued to the set every single night, but at sundown each Friday when she lights the candles, she always includes blessings for Rudy Vallee, Stoopnagle and Budd, Eddie Cantor, Jimmy Wallington, Jessica Dragonette, Joe Penner and—can you believe this?—*Father Coughlin!*

"Ma," I once asked her, "how can you say a blessing for Father Coughlin? He's an anti-Semite."

"So who's not?" Ma said.

She had me there.

But to get back to our family conference, "So who got a suggestion?" said Ma.

Pa stepped forward. Pa used to be a house painter back in the olden days when he was working and this is what he suggested: He'd take the hundred dollars and get his Plymouth back from the finance company. Then he'd drive around St. Paul looking for houses that needed

painting and when he found one he'd try to sell the
people a paint job.

Ma gave him a look. "Very intelligent," she said. "But
I got a question. When a house needs painting, it's because they ain't got money to paint. So how they gonna
pay you, Dr. I.Q.?"

Pa went into his patented sulk. That was his speciality:
injured silence. Whenever Ma gave him the whammy,
he just clammed up. Since Ma gave him the whammy
most of the time, he spent most of the time clammed up.
I was nearly eleven before I found out he wasn't deaf
and dumb.

Now my sister Libbie stepped forward. Libbie was the
one in the family who worked. She knocked down fourteen a week as assistant manager in kitchenwares at
Monkey Ward of which Ma let her keep two-fifty for
carfare and lunch. I only worked one day a week myself,
Saturdays at the Cut Price Grocery, but I came out
almost as well as Libbie. They paid me three dollars for
the day, but I told Ma I only got two so she only took
away one.

Libbie was twenty-four, four years older than me, but
we were pretty good buddies all the same. She slipped
me a dime every so often, and I kept telling her she
looked like Sylvia Sidney which made her very happy.
It was true in a way; she was short and hairy and cried
a lot.

Anyhow, Libbie stepped forward and said, "Mother,
I think I should have the money." Libbie was the only
one who called Ma "Mother" and Pa "Father." She also
wore white gloves every chance she got and spoke with a

broad *a* when she didn't forget. If the Prince of Wales happened to wander into Monkey Ward some day, Libbie meant to be ready.

"I think I should have the money," said Libbie, "so I can buy some decent clothes and get invited to nice parties and meet the right kind of people."

Ma gave Libbie a look. "Very intelligent," said Ma. "But I got a question. Who among your shlepper friends is gonna invite you to a nice party?"

Libbie couldn't think of an answer so naturally she started in crying. Ma turned to me next. "Well, breadwinner," she said, "I suppose you think you should have the money too?"

"As a matter of fact, I do," I said.

"This is gonna be good," said Ma. "All right, what will *you* do with the money?"

"This is gonna be better than you think," I said. "I will go to college."

What a bombshell! College? Who ever heard of such a thing? First of all, I was twenty years old and already two years out of high school. Second, the highest mark I ever got in high school was a B-minus and that was in tin shop. And third, even if you were a genius and came out of college with a lawyer degree or a doctor degree you'd still starve to death these days like everybody else.

They gave me a look, all of them, not just Ma, but Pa and Libbie too. They just stood and stared at me like they couldn't imagine where in the world I got such a nutty idea. To tell you the truth, it was *not* my idea. It was my cousin Albert's and he sprang it on me a couple of weeks earlier at the Sel-Dale Rec which I'll explain.

The Sel-Dale Rec is this pool hall on the corner of Selby and Dale where all the neighborhood guys hung out at night except of course on weekends when everybody was out prowling for nookie. Well, on the night I'm talking about, I walked into the Sel-Dale after supper as usual, and all the regulars were there, including my cousin Herbie, the prominent attorney who you know; my cousin Reuben who was thirty-five years old and still had a paper route; my cousin Willard who was going to be a millionaire any minute from chain letters; my cousin Pisher who got kicked out of the CCC for bedwetting; my cousin Bow-Wow who made a shaky living stealing dogs for the University medical school; my cousin August who came in seventy-eighth in a marathon dance last year; my cousin Kermit who ran the towel counter at the Y, the only fairy as far as I know in the entire family; and my cousin Albert.

And, of course, a lot of neighborhood guys who not only were not my cousins, but they weren't even Jewish. Selby Avenue got just about any nationality you can name, but we all live together with no trouble because we all got these two things in common: horniness and unemployment.

Anyhow, I walked into the Sel-Dale and everybody looked up hopefully for a minute thinking it might be a live one, but it was only me so they all turned away. Except my cousin Albert. He jumped to his feet, real excited. "Morris!" he hollered. "Where you been? I got to talk to you important!"

"So talk," I said.

"No. It's private," he said and dragged me to a little

booth in the back. It was no problem for Albert to drag me because he was a bull. He weighed 220 pounds and his shoulders were so wide that Foreman and Clark couldn't fit him. He had to have his suits tailor-made which is why he didn't have any. With that fantastic strength of his, Albert always wanted to be a professional fighter, but he was never able to find a manager willing to handle a heavyweight five feet one inch tall. So Albert worked a couple days a week unloading lettuce at Di Palma's produce house.

(Shortness, by the way, runs in my family. In fact, I got three grown cousins who can stand up straight under a card table. I myself at five feet six am known as the Gary Cooper of the family.)

But about Albert. He was, as I said, a bull and he looked like Nat Pendleton standing in a hole. But behind that tiny forehead was the busiest brain in St. Paul. He was all the time planning, scheming, plotting, driving, burning with ambition to make it. And he didn't just talk; he *did*. Like for instance the rest of us were always dreaming about how nice it would be to have a car. Well, Albert didn't dream. You know what he did? *He made a car!* It was part Ford, part Hudson, and part Maytag, but by God, it ran!

"All right, Albert," I said when we got seated in the booth in the back of the Sel-Dale, "what's so important?"

"Morris," he said and he was almost shaking with excitement, "I figured out why we're not making it. You know why? Because we are not using our *assets*."

This puzzled me. I quickly run through our assets in my mind, and all I could come up with was Albert's

Maytag Six and the Ingersoll pocketwatch I got for high-school graduation. "What assets?" I said.

"Think," said Albert. "What do we do better than anybody?"

"Hump," I said.

"Absolutely," said Albert. "We are no question the best humpers in the whole St. Paul. I am Number One and you are Number Two."

"Well, yes," I said, "but you rape most of yours. I don't think that should count."

It was true what I said. Not that Albert *meant* to rape them; it's just that he was so fantastically strong they usually fainted from a simple hug.

As for my own humping record, it was—I got to say it—incredible. I tell you this without bragging because I honestly can't take any credit. All that I was I owed to my cousin Crip; without him I would have been nothing.

I started chasing poon at fourteen like everybody else, and I got to admit that for the first year and a half all I accomplished was nutstrain. Then one day, just by chance, I was visiting my cousin Crip and all of a sudden I had the key.

Crip's real name actually was Walter, but he was crippled so much of the time that people naturally called him Crip, including his mother, my Aunt Ida. What he had was this calcium problem, either too much or too little, I'm not sure. Anyhow, his bones broke so easy you could hardly believe it. I mean all you had to do was give him an ordinary handshake and—crunch!—five busted fingers. If he sat down too fast in a wooden chair—wham!—the pelvis. When he went to bed he had to sleep flat on his back with his arms at his sides because if he turned over during the night, his arms would snap like chicken wings.

Naturally Aunt Ida took him to every doctor in the state of Minnesota and even to Chicago. The doctors were always happy to see him because at the very least he was good for an article in the medical journal, but nobody could figure out what to do. So Aunt Ida finally gave up and kept Crip at home on a goosedown sofa.

Crip was my age, twenty, but he'd never been to school. They tried sending him for a while when he was little, but it was no good. He never once came home without something busted. One time in kindergarten, I remember, a girl named Emily Dow tossed him a bean-bag and caved in his chest.

So they educated him at home. They got him a slew of books and they just let him go ahead at his own pace. Believe me, it worked out a lot better than if they'd sent him to school. I mean he was reading Shakespeare when the rest of us were still farting around with *The Little Engine That Could*. By the time he was twelve he was so well read that he started writing things of his own —poems, mostly, and they were great. He wanted to compose music too but he knew he dassn't because if he ever touched a piano it was good-by, fingers.

Well, you'd think a guy with bones like pretzels would be fairly gloomy, but not Crip. In fact I never met anyone happier. The bones didn't bother him because to tell the truth he never even felt it when they broke. But more important, he was doing what he liked best in the whole world, reading and writing. He would rave about a new book the way you and I would rave about a new broad, and he enjoyed writing even more than reading, especially writing poetry. Every time I came over he could hardly wait to show me his newest poem, and when I told him how much I liked it—and I always did—he'd grin and blush and wiggle all over with pleasure, except of course the parts that were in a cast.

Only once did I see Crip unhappy for any length of time. That was when he was fourteen and started getting horny. He wanted to get laid something awful, but naturally he couldn't. For him this would have been like jumping off the Foshay Tower. He suffered for almost a whole year, but finally he sublimated his sexdrive into poetry. (That's Crip's word: "sublimated." So is "sexdrive.") What he meant was instead of shagging girls, which he couldn't, he wrote these passionate love poems, which he could. He made up a whole bunch of romances with imaginary girls, all of them gorgeous, willing, and able. Why not? If you're inventing girls, you might as well do it right.

The poems were fantastic. Somehow he was able to make them sound filthy and beautiful at the same time. The language was perfectly clean, and the sentiments were very high-tone, but all the same, just listening to them you'd get a bone on. I mean these poems were such hot stuff that Crip had to tear them up when he finished them. He couldn't leave them around the house because Aunt Ida would throw a fit if she ever found them.

I'll give you an example in a minute, but first let me tell you how I happened by chance to get the key to a rich, wholesome sex life from Crip.

I was fifteen and a half at the time, and I was trying to stick it in a girl named Elaine Gonder at Central High. I was getting nowheres with Elaine, which wouldn't have bothered me too much—after all, I'd been striking out with everyone else too—but I knew for a fact that Duncan McCarthy and Galen Peterson had both gotten in. This wasn't just hearsay; it so happened I was looking over the transom in the locker room when each of them scored.

But I kept getting shut out with Elaine. I tried everything short of an ether cone, and the answer was always the same: no. "You don't love me," Elaine kept saying.

"Yes, I do," I hollered. "I am crazy about you, I swear on my mother!"

She wouldn't believe me.

Well, one day during the course of this Elaine fiasco I was visiting my cousin Crip and, as usual, he read me his latest love poem. He always had names for these imaginary girls he was writing about, and the title of the poem was always the name of the girl—*To Barbara,* for instance, or *To Beverly,* or *To Muriel.* The one he read me this day was called *To Elaine* and my ears perked up right away. The poem went like this:

TO ELAINE

Elaine, Elaine, oh sweet and fair,
Thy creamy skin, thy gleamy hair,
Thy marble brow, thy sapphire eyes,
Thy secrets I can but surmise.

Oh, where hast thou thy treasure hid?
Oh, dare I hope to ope the lid?
Oh, let me ope it once, Elaine,
Then let me ope it once again!

Well, I jumped straight up in the air. "Crip," I yelled, "don't tear up this poem. Give it to me."

"What for?" said Crip.

I told him.

He gave a frown. "You mean you're going to tell this broad that *you* wrote the poem?" he said.

I gave a frown. "It's okay, isn't it?" I said.

He gave a brave smile. "Sure, Morris," he said.

"Thanks, Crip," I said.

"Forget it," he said. "What are cousins for?"

I wanted to hug him then, but I knew better. "There's one more thing, Crip," I said. "The poem says *sapphire eyes*. That means blue, don't it?"

"So?" he said.

"So could you change it?" I said. "This broad's got brown eyes."

"Be glad to," said Crip. "What shade brown would you say they were?"

"Kind of liver colored," I said.

He shook his head. "Not good," he said. Then he thought for a while—not more than ten seconds—and came up with *russet*. That's how fast Crip could write poetry.

The next day I caught Elaine in the cafeteria at Central. "So I don't love you, huh?" I said. "Well, how do you like them apples?" I flang the poem down in front of her and walked away.

Within five minutes she was running around school like a crazy woman looking for me. Do I have to tell you what happened when she found me?

From that day on Crip was my secret weapon. Not,

mind you, that I used him all the time; in fact, not even most of the time. Because most of the time the action was with Swedish and Finnish housemaids who came to St. Paul direct from farms up in northern Minnesota and, believe me, when you are trying to un-hook the garters on a 180-pound squarehead who never went past the third grade, what you need is two extra arms, not poetry.

But often enough I'd run into a girl with (a) hot pants; and (b) a high-school education, and that's when I'd call on Crip. If the girl had a simple name like Mary or Doris, he could knock off a poem in half an hour. If she had an off-brand name like Ursine or Velva it took a little longer, but he always came through for me, God bless him. He was never too busy, too tired, or too bandaged. A real pal.

So, as you can see, my cousin Albert was dead right when he said that him and me were the top studs in town—him through brute strength and me through brain-power (Crip's). "All right, Albert," I said that night at the Sel-Dale Rec, "so we're the champs. So?"

"So we got to stop wasting our talent," said Albert. "No more screwing for pleasure."

"What then should we screw for?" I asked.

"Money," he said.

"Male whores?" I said, shocked.

"No, no, no," said Albert. "I mean we find a couple of rich broads, we boff them, they fall madly in love with us, and we marry them for their money."

I busted out laughing; I couldn't help it.

"What's wrong?" said Albert.

"So many things I don't know where to begin," I said. "But for openers, where are two losers like you and me gonna find rich broads?"

"That's easy," he said. "We'll enroll at the University of Minnesota."

I looked at him like the way I told you earlier my mother and father and Libbie looked at me. "Albert," I said, "it costs a fortune to go to the University."

"I checked," he said. "Tuition is a hundred bucks a year."

"Like I said, a fortune," I said. "Where you gonna get a hundred bucks?"

"Remember my ma's fur coat?" he said.

Did I remember Aunt Lena's fur coat? Everybody on Selby Avenue remembered it. It was a sensation when she got it way back in 1928—the first coat in the neighborhood anybody ever bought retail. But it had been at least five years since Aunt Lena used to parade that coat up and down Selby. When times got tough she put it away in cold storage to protect it from moths and thieves.

"What about the coat?" I said.

"I found where Ma hid the cold-storage ticket," said Albert. "I got the coat out and sold it for $100."

"Albert!" I gasped. That's all I could say.

"She'll never know," he said. "She's gonna leave it in storage till the Depression's over, and the Depression's never gonna be over."

"Okay, Albert," I said. "So you're all set. But where will I find $100?"

"That's a problem," he admitted. "But we'll work it out."

"How?" I said. "But even if by some miracle I do raise the money, your plan is still ridiculous."

"Why?" he said.

"I'll tell you why," I said. "You say first we boff these girls, then we marry them. True?"

"True," he said.

"Albert," I said, "if you marry a girl, she got to be Jewish."

"I know," he said. "So?"

"So Jewish girls don't put out," I said.

"Have you tried?" he said.

"Of course," I said.

"And what happened?" he said.

"They told me, 'I'm a Jewish girl. I don't put out,'" I said.

"Morris," he said, "shut up and listen carefully because now we come to the heart of my plan. Now, I myself have never boffed a Jewish girl either. In fact, I don't know anybody who has. We all tried, I guess, but we all ran into the same thing. They told us no, so we quit. Why? Because we believe the propaganda: 'Jewish girls don't put out.' But, Morris, think it through. Shicksas also say no at first, don't they? But do we quit? Of course not. We figure even if they mean it, they'll be grateful later . . . Well, Morris, why can't we give the same courtesy to Jewish girls?"

"Wait a minute," I said. "Are you suggesting that Jewish girls really want it?"

"Why not?" said Albert. "Aren't they human? Do you think a little tongue sucking is enough for them, a little grabass through a panty girdle? Don't you suppose they'd like to get their gun off just like everybody else?"

"I don't know," I said. "I never thought of it that way."

"Nobody has," said Albert. "And that is why the world is full of Jewish girls who are dying for a piece of tail. Well, Morris, you and I are gonna do something revolutionary: we're gonna give it to 'em."

I got thoughtful. As I've mentioned, Albert is no dope, and although his theory was something nobody ever figured out before, that didn't necessarily make it wrong. In fact, the longer I thought about it, the more sense it made.

But whether Albert was right or wrong, the big problem was where would I get a hold of $100? Which brings me back to my father's broken tailbone.

"I want the money to go to college," I said to my family and they all looked at me like my hair was on fire. I pressed on while I had them standing with their mouth open.

"In college I will have a chance to meet rich girls," I said, "and let's face it, the only way this family is ever gonna see any money is if I marry it."

Then I stepped back and waited for Ma to give me the whammy.

But she just stood and rubbed her chin for a couple minutes. "Makes sense," she said finally.

Libbie wasn't happy. "Wait a minute, Mother," she said. "If this is the way it's going to be, why shouldn't *I* go to college and meet a rich boy?"

"Because," said Ma, "you are too old for college boys, and you ain't no beauty into the bargain."

Libbie cried of course, and Ma did some more thinking. "Listen," she said, giving me a forefinger in the ribs, "no shicksas, you hear? Don't be like You-Know-Who."

You-Know-Who was my cousin Seymour whose name you couldn't even mention since he married a shicksa a few years ago. His family went into such conniptions like you wouldn't believe. They wailed and cried and said the prayer for the dead and sat shivah and ripped their lapels and poured ashes on their heads. I know because I had to bring them ashes from our furnace; they had an oil burner.

"No shicksas," I promised Ma.

"Another thing," said Ma. "Very important. Pick an ugly girl."

"What?" I said, puzzled.

"Use your head, Morris. Don't be like *him*," said Ma, pointing a thumb at Pa. "A pretty girl got plenty of dates, ain't she? Plenty of rich, high-class fellas. So what does she need with a cocker like you? Find an ugly."

"Okay, Ma," I said.

"But not just a *little* ugly," said Ma. "*Real* ugly."

"Okay, Ma," I said.

"All right, that's settled," said Ma.

"No," said Pa, "I don't agree."

"You don't *what?*" said Ma.

"After all, I am the one who broke the bone," said Pa. "I think I should have the money."

"No, Nathan dear," said Ma. "But I'll tell you what you can do."

"What?" said Pa.

"You can turn on Amos and Andy," said Ma.

Chapter Two

Freshman registration was on the Friday after Labor Day, and there we stood on the campus of the University of Minnesota, Albert and I, the Gold Diggers of 1936, and all around us we saw the other freshmen, every one of them beautifully dressed—the guys in tweed coats and flannels, the girls in angora sweaters and pleated skirts and saddle shoes. Albert and I were pretty spiffy ourselves. I was wearing my bar mitzvah suit, and Albert had on his zipper jacket from the Golden Gloves.

"Albert," I said, taking a gander at our new classmates, "do you think we look all right?"

"You worried?" he said.

"A little, maybe," I said.

"Morris," he said, taking me by both shoulders and looking straight in my eyes, "listen carefully to what I'm gonna tell you. It's true we ain't got clothes. Also we ain't got money, we ain't got looks, and we ain't got breeding. Therefore there is one thing we *got to* have."

"What?" I said.

"Confidence," he said.

He was absolutely right, of course. I mean how are you ever going to win a fight if you're covered with flop sweat before you start? So right there and then I made up my mind to shake off all my doubts and walk tall and keep smiling and talk loud. "You're absolutely right," I said to Albert.

He grinned and gave me a playful little punch I can still feel in damp weather, and off we went to see our freshman advisers.

Mine was named Mr. Harwood, a skinny man about thirty-five with chalk dust and no lips. "Hello," I said, "I am Morris Katz."

This news didn't excite him too much. Without looking up he pointed to a chair in front of his desk. I sat down. He opened a folder that had my name on it. "Mr. Katz," he said, "I have made a careful examination of your high-school records and your aptitude tests, and I have one question to ask: what in God's name are you doing here?"

I tried to think of an answer, like "How would you like a rap in the mouth?" but it turned out I didn't need it because he went right on talking.

"However," he said, "that is not properly my business. Since you have fulfilled the stringent entrance requirements of the University of Minnesota—which is to say you have a high-school diploma and one hundred dollars —my job is to help you make out a program of studies. What major are you interested in?"

"What's the easiest?" I said.

"Home economics," he said.

"What's the next easiest?" I said.

"It's between sociology and library science," he said. "To my certain knowledge nobody has ever flunked either."

"Which one got the most girls in it?" I said.

"Home economics," he said.

"No," I said. "I mean between sociology and library science."

"The *most* are in library science," he said. "However —and I think this is what you're getting at—the *best looking* are in sociology."

"I'll take library science," I said.

His eyebrows went up. "May one ask why?"

"I'd rather not say," I said.

"Come to think of it, I'd rather not know," he said. "Now, what other courses would you like to take?"

"It don't matter too much," I said. "I'm not expecting to be here long."

"I share this feeling," he said.

"Mr. Harwood," I said, "this is my first day at the University. I'm confused and I'm bewildered and what I need is help, not sarcasm. With respect, Mr. Harwood, why do you have to be such a schmuck?"

"You'd be surprised how many people ask me that," he said.

"No, I wouldn't," I said.

"I don't have an answer really," he said. "I can only point out that in addition to counseling several hundred freshmen each year, I teach three sections of composition, two sections of American lit, two of Shakespeare and one of Chaucer—plus I am supervisor of student publications and coach of the University chess team, making a work load of roughly twenty hours per day. Add to all this the fact that I have remained in the grade of instructor for the last twelve years, and possibly a picture begins to emerge. I offer this not in mitigation, you understand, but simply to clarify."

"How do I get another adviser?" I said.

"Don't bother. We're all schmucks," he said. "Now, about your other courses—"

"Whatever you think," I said. "I'll leave it up to you."

"I shall try to justify your confidence," he said and put me down for three credits in Dewey Decimals, three more in Shelving and Stacking, and then to add what he called "a leavening of culture" he gave me five credits in Remedial English and three in Birds of Minnesota.

"Good luck, Mr. Katz," said Mr. Harwood, "and welcome to the community of scholars."

When I met Albert later I found out he had exactly the same program as mine, except his adviser gave him Fingerprint Identification instead of Birds of Minnesota. "Well, what's the difference?" I said to Albert. "By this time next year we'll be married and laying around our own swimming pool."

"You bet your ass," he said and gave me another playful punch that stayed black and blue till Thanksgiving.

On Monday classes officially began. Albert picked me up at 7 A.M. and then we picked up Bruce Albright and Henry Leibowitz who I will tell you about in a minute. First let me explain about transportation.

St. Paul and Minneapolis are called the Twin Cities because they're right next to each other. But still it was ten miles from where Albert and me lived in St. Paul to where the University was in Minneapolis, so we needed some way to get back and forth. We had Albert's Maytag Six of course, so the car itself was no problem. The problem was where to find money for oil, grease, tire patches, spark plugs and parts that kept falling off. Gasoline was not an expense; that we siphoned from parked cars naturally.

What we needed were some paying passengers to ride with us and share expenses, so we'd spent last summer looking around the neighborhood for other guys who were enrolled at the U. It was slim pickings, I can tell you; who could afford foolishness like college? But finally we got lucky and found Bruce Albright.

Bruce, a Gentile, was going to med school, which he didn't especially want to, but his father, also a Gentile, insisted. His father was the most successful doctor in St. Paul, which was not surprising since he had the Jewish trade locked up. I'll tell you a curious fact you might not know: when Jews have operations—and, believe me, that's every chance they get—they always go to a Gentile doctor. They'll trust Jewish doctors with colds and constipation and everyday stuff like that, but when it comes to surgery, they yell for a Gentile every time.

The reason is simple: Jewish doctors are too young. Figure it out. If a Jew is, say, forty or fifty years old, he's almost sure to be an immigrant. So when could he have gone to med school? No, it's the *sons* who go to med school and, as my mother says, "You think I'm gonna lay there unconscious from chloroform and let some young punk cut me open who was making in his diapers a couple years ago?"

Well, that's how it is. Maybe as the years go by and Jewish doctors grow older, they'll get in on the big Jewish surgery boom, but as of 1936 it's a goyish monopoly.

But about Bruce. He was a big, strong guy about six feet four who never would have gone to med school if his father didn't make him. What Bruce liked was the outdoors—hunting, fishing, camping, canoeing, and all kinds of things Jewish mothers don't let you do. Only once did I manage to sneak away with Bruce. He took me fishing a few years ago at Bald Eagle Lake, and I want to tell you it was a day I'll never forget. The fishing itself was nothing to rave about—ten hours in a cloud of mosquitoes to catch eight little sunfish—but afterwards we went to a nearby farmhouse that Bruce knew and the old farmwife, for just one dollar, cleaned and fried our fish and served them to us with a dozen ears of golden bantam corn and a pitcher of fresh milk and a loaf of home-baked bread with plenty of country butter and after supper sucked us off.

Our other passenger, Henry Leibowitz, was also going to college because his father made him, but there was a big difference between Henry's father and Bruce's father. Bruce's father was loaded, but Henry's father was so poor I get hunger cramps just thinking about it.

Henry's father was called Reb Leibowitz, but he was a good long way from a rabbi. What he did was give Hebrew lessons to twelve-year-old boys, which got to be the lowest-paid profession in the world next to biting off chickens' heads in a carnival. The Reb usually charged ten dollars, never more than fifteen, to get a kid ready for his bar mitzvah, and can you imagine how long that took? Can you picture the resistance of a twelve-year-old boy who's spent the whole day in public school and now he can't go out to play ball because some old guy with bad breath is hocking him in Hebrew? And worse yet, the Reb didn't get paid till after the bar mitzvah, so whenever a kid cocked up the ceremony—about one out of three, I'd guess—there was no money at all.

Well, my house was poor and Albert's house was poor and nearly everybody's house was poor, but the Leibowitz house—that was POOR. What they ate I don't know, but I can tell you this: Reb Leibowitz, in full tfillin, couldn't have weighed a hundred pounds. Mrs. Leibowitz was smaller around than my thumb. Henry looked like a thermometer, and his brother Max who was five years older, looked like a thermometer with glasses.

Max, who I think was born with glasses, got nothing but A's in grade school and high school, and he ended up at the University with a full scholarship. I believe that's what kept Reb Leibowitz alive—not food, but pride in Max. "My Max! My Max!" the Reb would tell everybody. "He got the traditional Jewish love of learning!"

We all hated Max. "Why ain't *you* got the traditional Jewish love of learning?" our mothers would holler when we came home with a report card full of red ink. But of course it was toughest on Henry. He didn't have the traditional Jewish love of learning either, and he had to live in the same house.

(Incidentally, if you ask me, this so-called traditional love of learning is another Jewish myth, like Jewish girls don't put out. Some Jews love learning, some don't. Remember this: for every Einstein we got ten thousand dentists, and Barney Ross is by us a bigger hero than Louis Brandeis.

(No, love of learning is not what's kept the Jews going.

It's something else, something nobody knows. My cousin Albert thinks it's corn beef. Well, maybe.)

But back to Henry Leibowitz. Henry didn't want to bust his ass working for all A's but he was afraid not to. Once, I remember, when he came home from high school with six A's and just one single C, his father took a look, turned pale, and heaved all over the report card.

Well, Henry finally got so good at getting A's that he wound up with a full scholarship to the University just like his brother Max five years earlier, and Albert worked out a deal to drive him back and forth to school. Not for money naturally; where would Henry get money? But in exchange for transportation, Henry agreed to do Albert's homework every night and mine too which was a blessing, believe me, because it meant we wouldn't have to waste time studying and could concentrate on broads.

So anyhow, we got to school on this first day of the semester, and Albert and I went off to our eight-thirty class in Dewey Decimals. One look around the classroom and I knew Mr. Harwood hadn't been exaggerating about the number of girls who take library science; in fact, the only males in the whole class were Albert and me. We listened carefully to the roll call to find out who was Jewish, and we picked out four: Miss Bernstein, Miss Chodorov, Miss Zimmerman, and Miss Zucker.

Two of them we eliminated immediately: Miss Bernstein because she was good-looking, and Miss Chodorov because she didn't have a pledge pin on her sweater. We knew that any girl who didn't pledge a sorority was a poor girl, and a poor girl we needed like another nostril.

So it boiled down to Zimmerman and Zucker. "You got any preference?" Albert asked me.

It was like asking if you preferred the bulldog clap to a rusty nail in the foot. "No," I said.

"Me neither," said Albert. "Let's flip a coin. Heads I get Zimmerman, tails you get Zimmerman."

He took out a nickel and flipped it: tails.

So when class was over Albert went chasing after Zucker and I walked up to the other meatball and hit her with my very best smile. "Hi, there," I said. "Didn't we meet at the Cotillion last year?"

"I don't think so," she said. "I wasn't there."

"How come?" I said. "Couldn't you afford it?"

"Oh, sure," she said, "but I was touring Europe."

"Well, well," I said and rubbed my hands a little. "My name is Morris Katz," I said.

"Celeste Zimmerman," she said.

"How do you do?" I said. "You're not by chance any relation to A. M. Zimmerman?"

"He's my Daddy," she said.

"Well, well," I said again. It was getting better and better. A. M. Zimmerman just happened to own two dozen movie theatres in the Twin Cities, all of them jammed every night. I knew this for a fact because at one time or another I had snuck into every one of them and I never saw an empty seat.

"You got any brothers and sisters?" I said.

"No," she said.

"Well, well," I said for the third time. A sole heiress yet.

I took another look at her and to tell the truth, she

didn't look half bad. She had fine teeth, very white and even. True, they were buck teeth, but *white and even* buck teeth. Also, her eyes were a pretty shade of blue—not big, of course, but the glasses gave them a little extra size. Her skin was nice, no pimples and very few bristles, and her hair was okay. It wasn't any particular color, but at least you could see she didn't set it at home.

As for her figure, let's not go into it. Let's just say she had the regular number of parts and they all seemed to be in working order and her father owned twenty-four theaters and what the hell.

"Don't you just love library science?" I said.

"No," she said, "I hate it, but I'm too dumb to take anything else."

"Oh, come now," I said. "I don't believe that."

"Wait till you know me better," she said.

"There now is something I would like very much," I said. "Are you free tonight?"

"I'm free every night," she said. "Why?"

"If I can borrow my cousin's car would you like to go to the movies?" I said.

"Sure," she said. "But you don't need to bother your cousin. I have a car."

"Of your own?" I said.

"Yes," she said.

"Well, well," I said for the fourth time. Even her figure was beginning to look good.

"What time shall I pick you up?" she said.

"After supper," I said. "Six-thirty."

She was there right on the dot. I was waiting for her out in front of the house. I didn't want to introduce her to my family quite yet. I'm not ashamed of them, mind you. It's just that Ma has a habit of looking people over like she was picking out a chicken at a crooked butcher's, and I didn't want her scaring off Celeste before I had her firmly hooked.

"Hi, there," I said, getting into Celeste's car, a brand-new Oldsmobile, no less. "What movie would you like to see?"

"I don't care," she said. "What would you like?"

I had memorized the movies playing at all twenty-four of her father's theaters, figuring we could walk in free at any of them. "How about *The Petrified Forest* with Leslie Howard, Bette Davis, and introducing Humphrey Bogart?" I said.

"Saw it," she said.

"How about *My Man Godfrey* with William Powell and Carole Lombard?" I said.

"Saw it," she said.

And the same with the next twenty-two I named. We ended up at the Paramount, which A. M. Zimmerman did *not* own, seeing Jan Kiepura in *Give Us This Night*— fifty cents a ticket to hear a Polack sing, not to mention twenty cents for popcorn.

This meant I had to revise my schedule. I had planned to take it slow and easy with Celeste—first a couple of dates with just kissing, then a couple with kissing plus grabbing, and finally a poem from Crip and bye-bye cherry. But of course this plan was based on free movies. If I was going to have to buy theater tickets—and that's how it looked—I couldn't afford any such long courtship. I had to make my move tonight.

So right after Jan Kiepura I drove to the Grotto Look-out and parked the car. "Celeste," I said, wasting no time, "I love you."

"Why, for God sakes?" Celeste hollered.

I shrugged. "Go figure love," I said.

"But I'm not pretty and I'm not bright and I got a rotten shape," she said.

"I know," I said. "I love you anyhow."

"Do you expect me to believe that?" she said.

"Not right away," I said, "but let's kiss for a while and see how you feel."

"Well, that seems worth a try," she said.

So we kissed for a while till she got the hang of it, and then I took a hold of her tit. She didn't push me away so after a couple minutes I started sliding my hand under her skirt. She jumped like I'd stabbed her.

"Morris," she hollered, "what's the matter with you? I'm a Jewish girl."

"You didn't mind when I grabbed your tit," I said.

"That's different," she said.

"Why?" I said.

"That's rubber," she said.

"I love you," I said, and tried under the skirt again, but it was the same thing. She hollered she was Jewish and pushed me away. In fact, that's how it went all night —me yelling "I love you!" and digging for that crotch, her yelling she was Jewish and pushing me away. By midnight we were so sweaty and exhausted that both of us were glad to go home.

But still and all, I was satisfied with the night's work. Getting laid wasn't important. What was important was to convince her I loved her, or at least that such a weird thing might be possible. That I accomplished, I don't say she *believed* it, but she *wanted to,* it was obvious.

"Will I see you tomorrow night?" I said when we were parked in front of my house.

For a long time she didn't answer. She just sat and looked at me with a puzzled frown, trying to figure out if I could possibly be on the level. I didn't talk either. All I did was grab her hand and press my lips against her fingers.

"Okay," she said finally. "But remember, I don't put out."

"Good night," I said. "I love you."

I got out of the car and walked backwards into my house, throwing kisses every couple of feet. Celeste just sat and stared at me with her mouth open.

When I got inside the house everybody was asleep except my mother. She was exactly where I expected she'd be: in her nightgown peeking through the living room curtains. "Well, Morris," said Ma, looking out at Celeste who was still sitting glassy-eyed in her car, "nobody can say she ain't ugly."

"She is A. M. Zimmerman's daughter," I said, letting it drop kind of casual.

"Hoo-ha!" said Ma. She gave me the kind of look I don't see too much of—respect—and went back to peeking through the curtains.

Celeste still hadn't moved.

"She ain't paralyzed, is she?" asked Ma. "It don't matter, you understand. I'm just asking."

"No, she's thinking," I said.

"A slow thinker," said Ma. "Good."

After about ten minutes Celeste finally stirred, put the car in gear, and drove away.

"Well, sonny," said Ma, giving me another respectful look, "I got to hand it to you. *That* is a meatball."

"Thanks," I said. "So where do I sleep tonight?"

This was a question I had to ask every night which I'll explain.

There were two bedrooms in my house. One had a double bed, and that was where Ma and Pa usually slept. The other had twin beds, and that was where my sister Libbie usually slept. A long time ago when Libbie and I were little we both slept in that room but now of course we were too old for that, so on the nights when Ma and Pa were in their room and Libbie was in her room, I slept on the davenport in the living room.

But a lot of nights it didn't work that way. When Ma got real mad at Pa—not *ordinary* mad like every day, but *extra* mad—she wouldn't let him sleep in the double bed. So where could he sleep? Not with Libbie of course, and not with me either because the davenport wasn't even big enough for one. So here's what we did: Libbie went into the double bed with Ma, and Pa went to Libbie's room. This meant there was no need for me to use that narrow davenport because I could sleep on the other twin bed in Libbie's room.

So, as you see, we could never be sure about the sleeping arrangements till just before bedtime. It depended how mad Ma was.

"You're sleeping on the davenport tonight," said Ma.

"Okay," I said. "Good night."

"Listen," she said, "if you'd be more comfortable in Libbie's room, I'll be glad to throw Pa out of bed."

"No, no," I said. "I don't want you waking Pa."

"Why not?" said Ma. "He needs sleep maybe, your father?"

"But you'll have to wake Libbie too," I said.

"You're right," said Ma, giving me another respectful look, the third in one night, a new record. "What a smart boychik I got, thank God."

"Good night, Ma," I said.

Ma slapped her hand against her forehead. "What's the matter with me?" she said. "I don't have to wake *Libbie*. I'll wake *Pa. He'll* sleep on the davenport, *I'll* sleep in Libbie's room, and *you'll* sleep on the double bed."

"Please, Ma, the davenport is fine," I said.

"Shut up," said Ma, so I did because I knew if I kept arguing there'd be no sleep at all. So Ma went and rousted Pa. He was so confused for a minute that he started walking downtown to the library in his pajamas, but Ma finally shoved him onto the davenport and me into the double bed.

"Good night, my smart boychik," she said, tucking me in. "Good night, my last best hope."

Chapter Three

Here's what happened the next day.

Celeste was due to pick me up at six-thirty in the evening for our second date, so I got to my cousin Crip's house at four-thirty in the afternoon so he'd have plenty of time to write the poem. And it was a good thing I allowed the extra time because Crip had visitors when I arrived—two men in suits who were sitting in the living room with Crip and Aunt Ida and naturally a bowl of fruit in the middle. Aunt Ida believes a person will keel over dead if he goes as long as eight hours without fruit.

Crip gave me a wave and Aunt Ida said, "Hello, Morris. I want you should meet Dr. Sloan and Dr. Barnhart from the Mayo Clinic in Rochester."

The doctors put down their tangerines and shook hands. Then they went back to arguing with Aunt Ida. What they were doing was trying to persuade her to send Crip to Mayo because they had something new they wanted to try on him.

"Well, I don't know," said Aunt Ida. "He's been already four times to Mayo. So what good did it do?"

"Yes, I admit we've had no luck so far," said Dr. Sloan. "But this is an entirely new procedure."

"And it looks extremely promising," said Dr. Barnhart. "I do wish you'd let him come."

"Well, I don't know," said Aunt Ida again.

"Why don't we ask Walter what he thinks?" said Dr. Sloan.

"Who's Walter?" said Aunt Ida.

"That's me, Ma," said Crip.

"So what do you think, dolly?" said Aunt Ida.

"Well, I don't know," said Crip.

"See?" said Aunt Ida. "*He* don't know and *I* don't know and *you* don't know. So why shlep him around?"

"Will you at least think it over?" said Dr. Barnhart.

"All right, I'll think it over," said Aunt Ida.

"And you too, Walter," said Dr. Sloan to Crip.

"All right," said Crip. "Have you got any literature on this new procedure?"

Dr. Sloan's eyebrows went up. "Well, yes, but it's highly technical, Walter," he said.

"Don't worry about that," I said. "If it's writing, he'll understand it."

"Thanks, Morris," said Crip.

"You're welcome, Crip," I said.

"Very well," said Dr. Sloan, "we'll send the literature. And now we must be getting back."

They stood up.

"Take a few plums," said Aunt Ida. "It's a long trip to Rochester."

So the two doctors went back to Rochester, and Aunt Ida refilled the fruit bowl and left me alone with Crip. It's not a myth, incidentally, this myth about how Jews love fruit. They will kill for fruit. But here's a curious fact you might not know: they have no interest at all in green vegetables. I'll give you an example.

When I was in the second grade at Webster Elementary School the school nurse once gave us a lecture about the terrible diseases you get if you don't eat a green vegetable every single day. This panicked me pretty good, I want to tell you, because in my whole life I'd never even *seen* a green vegetable. So when I came home that afternoon I said, "Ma, I got to have a green vegetable every single day."

Ma gave me a look. "Who says?" she asked.

"The school nurse," I answered.

Which Ma figured she couldn't argue with. "Okay," she said, and since then she has given me a green vegetable every single day: a dill pickle.

But about Crip. Aunt Ida left us alone and I looked Crip over and was pleased to see what good shape he was in—one small walking cast on his left foot is all.

"Well, Crip," I said, "I sure hope those guys from Mayo are on to something good this time because nothing would make me happier than to see you up and around playing sports and screwing."

"Thanks, Morris," he said. "I know you mean it."

"I do," I said, and I did. Friends like Crip don't come in job lots.

"Well, Morris," he said, "I expect you want a poem."

"If it's not too much trouble," I said.

"My pleasure," he said. "What's her name?"

"Celeste," I said.

"Good," he said. "Plenty of rhymes for Celeste. Not like Rachel or Gladys. How soon do you need it?"

"No hurry," I said. "She's not due till six-thirty."

"What does she look like?" he said.

"She looks like Chicago after the fire," I said. "But that's not the point. She's A. M. Zimmerman's daughter."

"Hoo-ha!" he said.

"So you can see how important this is," I said.

"I didn't think Jewish girls put out," he said.

"We'll know tonight," I said.

"Toss me a pencil," he said.

"I'll *hand* you a pencil," I said and did. Then I sat quietly in a corner so I wouldn't disturb him.

The poem he wrote is right below, but before you read it I want to point out one thing. I'm not going to praise the poem because there's nothing I can say that you won't be saying yourself. All I want to point out is this: this poem, which by any reasonable standard got to be called a masterpiece, was composed by my cousin Crip in exactly 32 minutes. I swear this. Think about it as you read:

> *TO CELESTE*
> *Had I been blessed*
> *With wishes three*
> *The first should be,*
> *O fair Celeste,*
> *To be a rose*
> *Upon thy breast.*
>
> *Now canst thou name*
> *My next request?*
> *It is the same*
> *I do attest:*
> *Another rose*
> *On th'other breast.*

Herewith the third
(Mayhap the best):
To be a bird
Within thy nest.
(Aye, this methinks
Is splendidest.)

Hence fairy good,
Thy flight arrest.
These wishes three
Pray grant to me
For I would be
In fair Celeste,
In fair Celeste.

Well, I'm not going to pretend. I'll say it flat out. There were tears in my eyes when I read this poem. I'll admit it: I cried.

"Cut it out, Morris, will you?" said Crip, but I knew he was pleased all the same.

But if you think *I* got emotional, you should have seen Celeste. My God, what an exhibition! First tears, then laughter, then both together with hiccups, then hiccups with hysterics, then combinations of everything. I thought for sure I'd have to wrap her in wet sheets. But finally she calmed down.

"Okay, Morris," she said, "have your way with me." I had it.

"Is it over?" she said.

"Yes," I said.

"Frankly I don't see what everybody's raving about," she said.

"It'll get better," I said.

"I certainly hope so," she said.

And in fact it did get better, which I'll tell you about later, but I don't want to get ahead of my story. All I'll say now is my cousin Albert was absolutely right about Jewish girls. They are wild for nookie; all you got to do is show them the way.

Speaking of Albert, let me fill you in quickly on what he was doing. He took out Miss Zucker the same night I took out Celeste, and for a while he thought he was home free. He took her to a movie and afterwards parked by Lake Phalen and began hugging her and she passed out within minutes from lack of oxygen. So far, so good. Then he went to pull her girdle off, and here is where the trouble began. The girdle turned out to be an entire foundation garment, or maybe even a corset, and before Albert could figure out how it worked Miss Zucker came to and started letting out such screams that passing cars were pulling over to the side of the road; they thought it was a fire engine. So of course he had to take her home where Miss Zucker gave the maid instructions to pour hot water on Albert if he ever showed up again.

"Tough, Albert," I said when he told me the story.

"Well, it wasn't a total loss," said Albert. "I banged the maid."

But to get back to Celeste. She quickly developed a taste for humping—not a talent, mind you, just a taste—and before the first week was over she was following me around like a dog. So on Saturday night I made my next move.

"Celeste," I said, "don't you think it's time you met my folks and I met yours?"

"Well, I'm in no hurry," Celeste said. "I hear your mother is ghastly."

"Who told you?" I said.

"My father," she said. "He said your mother is a bitch on wheels and your father is so dumb he can't find his ass with both hands."

"Where does he know them from?" I said.

"From way back," she said.

"I see," I said. "Did he say anything about me?"

"Oh, yes," she said. "He said you were a slimy little fortune hunter and I can't ever see you again."

"What did *you* say?" I said.

"I drank a bottle of iodine," she said.

"Well, Celeste," I said, "you can't keep drinking iodine every night. I better meet your father and explain the facts."

"What facts?" she said.

"I am no fortune hunter," I said. "I love you."

"Oh, Morris, he'll never believe that," she said. "I'm having plenty trouble myself."

"How can you doubt me?" I said. "Read the poem."

"I can't," said Celeste and all of a sudden started to giggle.

"Why can't you?" I said. "And what's so funny?"

"Promise you won't get mad," she said.

"About what?" I said.

"Well," she said, "that poem is so brilliant and so wonderful and so thrilling—"

"Yes?" I said.

"That I submitted it to *L'Etoile du Nord*," she said.

"What's that?" I said.

"The literary magazine at the University," she said.

"Wait a minute," I said. "*You* submitted *my* poem?"

"Under your name, of course," she said.

"But you never asked me," I said.

"I was afraid you'd say no," she said.

"Damn right I'd say no," I said.

"See? I knew it," she said. "Morris, you musn't be selfish. The world needs beauty."

"When did you submit the poem?" I said.

"Yesterday," she said.

"So you haven't heard from the magazine yet," I said.

"I won't hear. *You* will," she said.

"What's the name of this magazine again?" I said.

"*L'Etoile du Nord,*" she said.

I made a careful note of it because first thing Monday morning I was going over there and take the poem back. I couldn't do a rotten thing like that to my friend Crip—let his poem be published under my name. It was enough he was getting me laid; he didn't have to get me famous too.

So I said no more to Celeste about the poem; that problem would be taken care of on Monday. Right now I had a more urgent problem to take care of: A. M. Zimmerman. If I couldn't get him on my side, the whole project was in the toilet.

"Celeste," I said, "I want to talk to your father as soon as possible."

"No, Morris," she said, "let me do it my way. I'll keep trying to kill myself and he'll come around eventually."

"That's no good, Celeste," I said. "Some day he might not stop you."

"Yes, that could happen all right," she said.

"So how's about if I come over tomorrow?" I said. "What time do you eat on Sunday?"

"Brunch is eleven o'clock," she said.

I didn't know what brunch was but I didn't ask because I figured my sister Libbie, who keeps track of high society, would tell me. She did. Brunch is lox and bagel, except in silver dishes.

So on Sunday morning I got up early and caught a nine o'clock streetcar because it was a good long trip from where I lived to Celeste's house in fancy uptown Minneapolis. I made it a few minutes before eleven and walked up on the porch past a big lawn with statues and rang the doorbell.

Celeste answered. "Hi, there," I said.

"Let's go in and get it over with," she said.

She led me inside the house which I won't even try to describe. All I'll say is I never saw such a house before except in MGM movies with Norma Shearer.

Celeste's mother and father were in the dining room. There was also a maid and butler laying out silver dishes. I'd seen lots of maids before but never a butler except, of course, in those same Norma Shearer movies.

Mrs. Zimmerman was a lumpy woman who looked like Celeste, only with wrinkles. Mr. Zimmerman was a fat, purple-faced man in a cashmere suit that cost more than some people pay for a house.

"Mummy, Daddy," said Celeste, "I'd like you to meet Morris Katz."

"How do you do?" I said.

Nobody answered. Mrs. Zimmerman looked at me for a second and bit her lip. Mr. Zimmerman said, "Let's eat."

There was no conversation at brunch either. Mrs. Zimmerman would give a sniffle once in a while, but Mr. Zimmerman just kept his head bent over his plate, stoking his face with both hands. To be honest, I didn't mind the no conversation. I'd never had such fancy groceries in my life.

When Mr. Zimmerman had finished his twelfth or fifteenth helping, he pushed his plate away and turned to me. "Okay," he said, "we'll talk in the library."

This puzzled me for a second because I knew the library was closed on Sundays, but he meant his own. So I followed him toward a set of double doors—he stopped for a minute on the way to give his wife a pat; she was crying pretty hard by now—and then we went into a big room full of leather-bound books stacked floor to ceiling. A good thing Celeste was taking library science.

"Well, you certainly got a lot of nice books," I said.

"Books are bullshit," he said. "Sit down and shut up. I'll do the talking. Want a cigar?" He handed me a mahogany box.

"Thanks," I said, taking one. "I'll smoke it later."

"Bullshit," he said. "You'll *sell* it later. Get a good price. They're four bits retail."

I made a note of it.

"Let's not waste time with bullshit," he said. "Let's get right to the point which is this: it don't bother me that somebody's trying to marry Celeste for her money. Why else would they marry her? But she can do better than *you*, for Christ sakes. With her money she should get at least a German Jew, not a Litvak from the low-rent district."

"So where did *you* come from?" I said.

"Never mind *from*," he said. "Look at me *now*—successful, respected, feared, a president of B'nai Brith, a man with a butler. Who the hell are *you*, horning in around here?"

"I am the choice of your daughter, that's who," I said.

"Leave her out of this," he said. "She don't know her ass from a hot rock, especially since you showed up. Somehow you got her hypnotized—what *hypnotized?* You're diddling her, that's simple—so as a practical man I got to consider the possibility you might pull it off. Well, let me tell you something before this thing goes too far. In case you got a notion the money's gonna fall in your lap if you marry Celeste, forget it. You'll get *nothing*."

This made me thoughtful, you can be sure. "*Nothing?*" I said.

"Not a penny," he said. "Oh, I might give you a job maybe. But I pay thirty a week tops and you'll work your balls off, I guarantee you. Remember, I got two dozen theaters and they're open till eleven every night. So, Mr. Fortune Hunter, here is the big jackpot you're chasing: for sixteen hours a day you'll work your balls off, and at night you'll come home and find Celeste . . . What's the matter, kid? Something on your mind?"

I'll tell you what was on my mind. When you threaten a guy like me with thirty dollars a week it's like threatening a dog with meat. Why, for Christ sakes, for thirty a week I'd have married a pregnant Chinese midget with one short leg!

"Mr. Zimmerman," I said, "I don't know why you keep talking about money. I love Celeste and that's all that matters."

"Bullshit," he said. "You gonna stay away from my daughter?"

"No," I said.

"Then you're a bigger putz than I thought you were," he said. "Shall we join the ladies?"

So we went back into the other room where Celeste and her mother were cracking their knuckles. "Nu?" said Mrs. Zimmerman, giving an anxious look at Mr. Zimmerman.

"He won't quit," said Mr. Zimmerman.

Mrs. Zimmerman threw her face on the table and shrieked, but Celeste gave me a big smile.

"Well, Mrs. Zimmerman," I said, "I'm sorry you and Mr. Zimmerman feel this way. I can only hope you will get to like me better because if you like me or not you are going to have me for a son-in-law."

"Not while there's a breath left in my body," said Mr. Zimmerman, and Mrs. Zimmerman cried so hard she slid out of her chair. Mr. Zimmerman picked her up and took her away somewheres—to a recovery room maybe.

"Well, Celeste," I said, "how's about coming over to meet *my* folks now?"

"Do I have to?" she said.

"Yes," I said, and we drove over to St. Paul and got to my house just as Pa was reading the last few stanzas of Itzik Fishel's new poem which I'll explain.

Ma doesn't know how to read, not even Yiddish. She won't admit it, of course. She always says she can't find her glasses, but she can't read and that's a plain fact. So every Sunday Pa goes out and gets the Sunday edition of the *Jewish Daily Forward* and reads it out loud to Ma. First he reads the news stories which naturally are all about pogroms and strikes because the *Forward* is not only Jewish, it's also socialist. Then he reads the editorials —against pogroms, for strikes—and for the grand finale he reads the latest poem by Itzik Fishel, who is called "The Sweet Singer of the Sweat Shops" and who writes a long poem every week where he hollers about the downtrodden workers and the rotten bosses.

He's a real fire-eater, this Itzik Fishel, and Pa puts everything he's got into the reading—yelling, rolling his eyes, waving his arms. It's not so much that Pa likes the poetry, but it's the only time in the week when he's allowed to raise his voice.

Celeste got pretty nervous when she saw Pa carrying on, but I didn't want to interrupt his one big moment of the week so I waited till he was finished. Then I introduced Celeste to Ma and Pa. Libbie wasn't there.

"How do you do?" said Celeste.

"How do you do?" said Pa.

"Sit down," said Ma. "You want a bottle pop?"

"No, thank you," said Celeste.

"I knew your father in the old days," said Ma.

"Yes, I know," said Celeste.

"He always had snot hanging from his nose," said Ma.

"Is that so?" said Celeste.

"How's your mother?" said Ma. "She still have fits?"

"Not too often," said Celeste.

"Give her my regards," said Ma.

"Thank you," said Celeste.

"Where's Libbie?" I said.

"You won't believe it," said Ma. "She's out with a fella."

"No kidding," I said, surprised. "Who?"

"A new one she found someplace," said Ma. "He got a funny name."

"Jonathan Kaplan," said Pa.

"Yeh, Jonathan Kaplan," said Ma. "Who ever heard of naming a boy after a apple?"

"Libbie's my sister," I said to Celeste.

"She's about your size," said Ma to Celeste, "so if you got any dresses you don't need—"

"Well, I guess we'll be moving along," I said.

"I'd like that," said Celeste.

"You missed most of Itzik Fishel," said Pa. "You want I should read it again?"

"No, he don't," said Ma. "Good-by, Celeste. Remember about the dresses."

So Celeste and I went out and spent the afternoon driving around the countryside. It was beautiful Indian summer weather, so we stopped for a while at Powderhorn Park and got laid in a pile of leaves. Afterwards we saw Jack Oakie, Ann Miller, and Kenny Baker in *Radio City Revels* at A. M. Zimmerman's Bijou Theater for free, and then Celeste brought me home. All in all, a thoroughly successful day.

Chapter Four

I was still grinning the next morning when Albert picked me up for school. "Good weekend, huh?" he said, noticing my grin.

"Let me put it this way," I said. "I think I'm engaged."

"Mazeltov, Morris," he said, and gave my arm a squeeze that ripped the sleeve like paper.

"How about you?" I said. "Any dates this weekend?"

"Two," he said.

"Good," I said.

"No," he said. "Saturday she was so fat I couldn't find it, and Sunday I drew a dyke."

"Well, hang in there, Albert," I said. "Remember the old confidence."

"You bet," he said, giving my other arm a squeeze, and now I had a sleeveless jacket.

Then we picked up Bruce Albright and Henry Leibowitz and drove to school. As soon as we got there I went to the basement of the journalism building where the *L'Etoile du Nord* office was so I could get Crip's poem back.

In the office were these two fairies reading manuscripts and drinking tea in little thin cups under a picture of somebody named Hart Crane. Behind them was a closed door marked "EDITOR."

"Yes?" said the first fairy.

"I got to see the editor," I said.

"She has somebody with her at the moment," said the first fairy. "But I'm sure she won't be long. Would you care to wait?"

"Okay," I said.

"Sit any-old-where," said the second fairy. "We're very slap-dash here."

"Lapsang Souchong?" said the first fairy, holding out a teapot.

"No, thanks," I said.

"I'm Lance Berman," said the first fairy.

"I'm Claude Applebaum," said the second.

"How do you do?" I said, but I sure as hell didn't give them my name. That's all I needed: fruits on the phone every night.

So I just found a place to sit and sat down and looked through some old issues of the *L'Etoile du Nord* which was a small magazine with splinters in the paper and smeary ink and a lot of what they call free verse. Now, I don't pretend to be an expert, but to me the difference between free verse and my cousin Crip's poetry is the difference between chicken shit and chicken salad.

But luckily I didn't have to read too long because pretty soon the door marked "EDITOR" swung open and to my surprise out walked Mr. Harwood, my freshman adviser.

Lance and Claude jumped up when they saw him. "Well?" they said to him.

"No," he said to them.

"Oh, drat!" they said, and stamped their foot.

Then Mr. Harwood noticed me sitting there. "Well, well," he said. "I had no idea pornography was among your meager talents."

"What are you talking about?" I said.

"Your poem," he said. "I use the term loosely."

"What do you know about it?" I said.

"More than I wish, Mr. Katz," he said. "I am, as I believe I told you, the faculty supervisor of student publications."

"My gracious!" screamed Lance, grabbing my sleeve. "Are *you* Morris Katz?"

I nodded, not knowing what the hell.

"He's here! He's here! Morris Katz is here!" screamed Lance and Claude together, jumping up and down and clapping their hands and running through the door marked "EDITOR."

"Actually, I'm rather sorry I can't allow your doggerel to run," said Mr. Harwood to me. "As undergraduate effusions go, yours is almost readable. But it is, I'm afraid, far too spicy for the Christ-bitten clods who run this university. You do understand?"

"Sure," I said because at last I did understand and I was tickled pink. Mr. Harwood was telling me that he wouldn't let the magazine publish my poem—I mean *Crip's* poem—because it was too dirty. Which solved my problem completely.

"Well, good-by, Mr. Katz," said Mr. Harwood. "Will I be seeing some more of your work?"

"I doubt it," I said. "I'm thinking of quitting poetry."

"Pursue that thought," said Mr. Harwood and left, the prick.

Then I started to leave myself, but at this moment the editor came tearing out of the door marked "EDITOR" followed by Lance and Claude. The editor was a girl about nineteen or twenty, not tall, not short, with a pretty face and pretty hair and a first-class pair of knockers. She grabbed my hand and squeezed it hard and looked right into my eyes. "Mr. Katz," she said, "I am honored to meet you—deeply, deeply honored. You're not leaving, I hope?"

I shook my head. I wasn't going anywheres, I was staying right here because I had just come down with a big case of the hots for this lady editor. In fact, in my whole life I had never come down with such big hots in such a big hurry. And it was more than simple hots. I felt all kinds of feelings, all good. I felt happy and foolish and excited and smiley and lucky, all rolled into one.

For a second I got scared. Could this be *love*? If so, I was going to make tracks in a hurry. Because love I needed like I needed a wart on my nose, especially right now when Celeste Zimmerman, the heiress, was all plucked and trussed and ready for delivery.

But how could it be love? Me, Morris Katz, the master cocksmith from Selby Avenue, was I the kind of farfel-head who goes around falling in love at first sight with strange broads? Ridiculous.

It was just a case of oversized hots, that's all, and I saw no reason why I shouldn't give it a go.

"No, I'm not leaving," I said to the lady editor.

"Oh, splendid," she said. "Mr. Katz, promise me something."

"Anything," I said.

"Will you write some more poems for the magazine?" she said.

"My pleasure," I said.

Lance and Claude let out a cheer, and the girl gave me such a smile that I almost came on my leg. "Let's go into my office," she said.

If she'd said, "Let's go into the University boiler," I'd have followed her just as fast. I really felt something big for this broad. The hots, of course, but something extra too. For a second I got scared again, but it passed.

She sat down at her desk and I sat on the other side. "Mr. Katz," she said, "poetry is my life."

"Call me Morris," I said.

"Oh, may I?" she said.

"Why not?" I said.

"Morris," she said, "poetry is my life. To find a talent such as yours—such a combination of paganism and lyricism, such elfin conceits, such grandeur alongside such whimsy, as though Herrick and Milton were somehow combined, or Marvell blended with Keats—"

"Listen," I said. "What are you doing tonight?"

"Nothing," she said. "Why?"

"Would you like to go out with me?" I said.

"You mean it?" she said. "*You* want to take *me* out?"

"I'd like to see anyone stop me," I said.

"I'm honored," she said. "Deeply, deeply honored."

"Good," I said. "You haven't got a car, have you?"

"No," she said.

"Never mind," I said. "I'll scare one up somewheres. Is seven o'clock all right?"

"Fine," she said. "I'm in the women's dorm. Ask for me at the desk."

"In that case I better have your name," I said.

"Of course," she said. "How silly of me."

"So what is it?" I said.

"Bridget O'Flynn," she said.

"Oy," I said.

Chapter Five

My excuse is this: how can a person recognize love when they never caught it before?

I'm talking about Bridget O'Flynn. What I had for her was nothing as uncomplicated as the hots. It was love, no question, and a heavy case into the bargain, but I didn't realize it till later that night. I should have known right away, I guess, but I didn't. Albert did.

I ran to find Albert as soon as I left the *L'Etoile du Nord* office. "Albert," I said, "I got to borrow your car tonight."

"What for?" he said. "I thought Zimmerman had a car of her own."

"It's not Zimmerman," I said. "I just met a sensational new broad."

"Rich?" he said.

"I don't know," I said.

"Jewish?" he said.

"Sure," I said. "She's one of the O'Flynns from Minsk."

"No," said Albert.

"No what?" I said.

"No car," he said.

"How come?" I said.

"Look how you look," he said. "You are rosy like an

apple and your eyes are double size and you can't stop grinning."

"So?" I said.

"So I have seen those signs before," he said, "and they can only mean one thing: love, you schmuck."

"That's ridiculous," I said. "I want to bang this broad is all."

"Not in my machine," he said. "I ain't gonna provide the vehicle for you to fuck away the Zimmerman millions."

I argued some more because it really did sound ridiculous, what Albert said, but he was a rock so I had to go look for someone else with a car. After striking out with about a dozen guys, I finally tried Bruce Albright who didn't have a car but his father the doctor did.

"Bruce," I said, "do you think you could get your father's car tonight?"

"I doubt it," said Bruce. "He needs it at night in case the hospital calls."

"Couldn't he take a streetcar?" I said. "This is important."

"You got some broads?" Bruce said.

"Just one," I said.

"For both of us?" Bruce said.

"As a matter of fact, only me," I said.

"So what do *I* do?" Bruce said. "Fan your ass?"

"Actually," I said, "what I had in mind was you hang around the pool hall while I take the car."

"In your hat," Bruce said.

"Bruce," I said, "if you saw this broad, you'd do it."

"Morris," he said, "I have seen your broads and in my

opinion they are not worth somebody dying of a ruptured appendix while my father waits for a streetcar."

"You haven't seen Bridget," I said.

He gave me a funny look. "Bridget who?" he said.

"O'Flynn," I said.

He got red in the face. "Is that who you think you're gonna boff tonight?" he said.

"Not *think*," I said. "This is a lead pipe."

He got red in the neck besides the face. "Listen," he said, "it so happens I have been trying to pin Bridget O'Flynn for two semesters."

"You mean fraternity pin?" I said.

"Yes," he said. "For your information I love that girl. In fact, I'd marry her in a minute if she'd have me."

"Oh-oh," I said.

"So you keep the hell away from her," said Bruce. "You hear me?"

"I hear you," I said, and you'd think that would have been the end, true? Two clear warnings: one from Albert and one from Bruce. So what did I do next? I went and found Celeste Zimmerman.

"Celeste," I said, "I'm sorry but I can't go out with you tonight. I got a job."

"Oh, heck," she said. "Well, never mind. I'll pick you up when you finish work."

"I don't finish till morning," I said. "I'm a night watchman at the First National Bank."

"Well, this is a fine how-do-you-do," she said. "How long is this job gonna go on?"

"Not very," I said. "I'm just trying to raise a little money so I can take you to nice places."

"I don't want to go to nice places," she said. "All I want is to get in the back seat and you-know."

"We will," I said. "Real soon."

"Don't forget," she said.

"By the way," I said, "since you're not going anywheres tonight, can I borrow your car?"

(You see? You see what kind of madness I was in the grip of? No risk was too big, no trick was too dirty, and still I didn't realize what it was, this thing I had for Bridget O'Flynn.)

Even when I picked her up at seven o'clock in the women's dorm, I didn't realize what it was. True, I felt a little goofy when I saw her; in fact I wanted to laugh right out loud. But that didn't seem like anything to get alarmed about.

"Hello, Morris," said Bridget and sure enough I busted out laughing. Not little bitsy chuckles either; big ho-ho-ho's.

"Is anything wrong?" she said.

I shook my head and kept on laughing. Anything *wrong?* Never in my life had anything been so *right.*

"Shall we go?" she said, giving a nervous look at the house mother who was giving a nervous look at me.

So I managed to stop laughing except for a giggle that got loose every now and then, and I put Bridget in the Oldsmobile I had borrowed from Celeste and drove down to the River Bank and parked. I pushed the seat back and stuck one hand around Bridget's shoulder and the other one on her knee.

"Morris," she said, taking my hand off her knee. "Bruce

Albright phoned earlier and said you were going to try to seduce me tonight."

"There's a pal," I said.

"I would be terribly disappointed if that's all you had in mind," she said.

"You would, huh?" I said.

"Of course," she said. "This is the first time I've ever been close to a real poet. There are so many questions I'd like to ask."

"Well, okay," I said. "But don't be surprised if I sound just like a regular person."

"What I want to know primarily is this," she said. "What makes a poet? I mean beside talent and sensitivity. And empathy naturally. And of course the gift of imagery and the thirst for beauty and the questing heart."

"That about covers it," I said. "And may I say you sure know your onions about poetry?"

"How much agony is necessary to the creative process?" she said.

"A whole lot," I said.

"So it's true what Shelley says," she said. "*They learn in suffering what they teach in song.*'"

"Old Shelley's right on the nose as per usual," I said.

"I'll bet he's your favorite poet," she said.

"That's right," I said. "He's Number One in my book."

"I was sure of it," she said. "What do you think of Milton?"

"Milton who?" I said.

"John Milton," she said.

"Number Two," I said.

"My feeling exactly," she said. "Don't you think it's a shame he's so neglected today?"

"Well, you know the public," I said. "All the time new thrills."

"How true," she said. "Where do you rate Wordsworth?"

"Number Three," I said. "You about through asking questions?"

"Just one more," she said. "You're Jewish, aren't you?"

I knew from experience there was no use lying when they asked this one. You might be able to explain away your big hook nose, but once the pants came off, the cat was out of the bag for sure. "Yes," I said.

"How lucky for you," she said.

I gave her a look.

"To be one of the People of the Book," she said. "To live for art, for culture, and for social justice."

"Yup, that's what we live for," I said, thinking of a few examples: my cousin Albert, for instance, and Lepke Buchalter, and a kid named Heshie Stein from my neighborhood who used to fart in a Mason jar every morning before school, seal the lid real quick, and then let it loose in the cafeteria at lunchtime.

But what the hell, if Bridget thought Jews were the cat's meow, why complain? Would I have been better off if she called me "Sheeny" and spit on my gabardine?

"And how lucky for me too," said Bridget, looking at me all big-eyed and panty. "To be in the company of such a man—poet, civil libertarian, sensualist, Jew—why, it's a dream come true!"

"The hand's going back on the knee now," I said.

"All right," she said. "But I think you should know I'm a virgin and will resist."

"Well, let's see what happens," I said.

So I put my hand on her knee and gave her a kiss, just a small kiss, exploratory you might say. No tongue, no pressure, just lips lightly on lips for a count of five. Not more than five, I'm sure, because all of a sudden I couldn't stand it. I took my lips off hers and my hand off her knee and jumped away, as far away as I could get, all the way over to the corner of the seat behind the steering wheel. Because now, finally, I knew what I should have known from the beginning. It was love.

Well, if I tell you I was surprised, I'd be short-changing you. I was just plain poleaxed, that's what I was. *Love? Me?* How could it happen?

But it *had* happened, and no mistake. So what was I going to do about it? Well, that didn't take much thinking. I was going to stop right now. Take Bridget home, give her a firm handshake, and never look back. What else *could* I do?

So I reached for the key to start the car and all of a sudden a new thought hit me. Or let's be honest: I thought it was a thought but it wasn't. Like any other schmuck in love I began to con myself. I'll dump Bridget, I told myself. Don't worry, I'll dump her. But what's the hurry? What's it going to hurt if I wait a couple days? Or even a couple weeks? Don't I deserve to enjoy a little? Have I got such a great life to look forward to with that meatball Celeste? Ain't I entitled to pile up a few memories before I begin my stretch?

You see? That's what you do when you're in love. You

sell yourself horseshit and call it kreplach. And you don't know the difference, that's the funny part. Anyhow, I didn't. Don't worry, I'll get rid of her next week, I told myself, and I took her in my arms.

What happened next you can believe or not, suit yourself, but it's the God's truth. I took her back in my arms and kissed her and right away I could tell there was absolutely nothing between me and the goal line. Not only was she not resisting, but she was *helping*. So what did I do? I stopped, that's what.

That's right. I took one hand off her knee and the other off her tit and just sat back and held her gently, not even kissing, just holding gently and every once in a while giving her hair a sniff. That's all: just holding and smelling hair for maybe half an hour.

"Morris," said Bridget after a while, "did you forget what you were going to do?"

"No," I said, "but somehow, don't ask me why, this is all I want right now." Which was the truth.

"You're very sweet," said Bridget.

"You are Milky Way and Snickers together," I said. "Tell me about yourself."

"What do you want to know?" she said.

"Are your folks well fixed?" I said, thinking maybe if she was a rich shicksa it might put a whole new face on the situation.

"I never knew my mother and father," she said. "I was raised by the sisters."

"Whose sisters?" I said.

"The nuns at the Convent of the Sacred Heart," she said.

I groaned. Here's how my mother felt about nuns: if she ever happened to see one on the street, she made a circle three times, said *Shma Yisroel* and ran to kill a chicken.

"I was a foundling actually," said Bridget. She was full of good news, this broad. "But I wouldn't have traded my upbringing for anyone's in the world. It was Sister Mary Frances who taught me to love poetry. Do you know I was only two years old when she had me reciting *Invictus?* You're familiar with *Invictus,* of course."

"Who ain't?" I said.

"Oh, Morris," said Bridget, "I can hardly wait till you meet Sister Mary Frances. You two will adore each other."

Sure, I thought. And Ma will adore her too. Maybe we can all get together and recite *Invictus* over a glass of Manischewitz.

"But enough about me," said Bridget. "It's you who are the fascinating one. Tell me what you're writing at present."

"A poem," I said. "What else?"

"Oh, Morris!" she said. "When can I see it?"

"Tomorrow night," I said.

"Oh, Morris!" she said again and she kissed me again and it was so wonderful I didn't want to let go. I just wanted to sit and kiss her all night. Not *bang* her; *kiss* her. There was still no horniness. If love is supposed to get it up for a guy, I had the wrong kind.

But I tore myself loose after about fifteen minutes because I knew if I kept up this insane kissing it would be so late when I got back to St. Paul that Crip would be fast asleep and where would I get a poem? So I took Bridget back to the dorm, made a date for seven to-morrow night, and headed for Crip's.

Chapter Six

There was a surprise waiting for me when I got to Crip's house: he wasn't home. Aunt Ida and Uncle Shimen were there spitting out seeds from a bunch of Tokays, but Crip was gone.

"Gone where?" I said.

"Rochester," said Aunt Ida. "He read the new stuff from the Mayo Clinic and he decided to take a chance."

"How long will he be there?" I said.

"A week, maybe two, who knows?" said Aunt Ida.

"Well, give him my best wishes for a total recovery and especially a swift return," I said, and went home wondering how I was going to stall Bridget tomorrow.

At home on this night of surprises I found still another surprise. In fact, several. First of all the lights were on in the living room. Usually at this hour on Monday night the only light you could see was from the dial on the radio where Ma was listening to the "Lady Esther Serenade." But tonight not only the table lamp was lit, but the floor lamp and the overheads too. And—get this—the radio was *off*.

But that wasn't all. Everybody was sitting in the living room all dressed up—Ma, Pa, Libbie, and a guy with a moustache and one gold tooth. This guy had on a greenish tweed bi-swing suit with leather buttons and patch pockets. Pa had his suit on too and even a tie. Ma was decked out in the brown silk she usually saves for meetings of the Jewish Free Burial Society, and as for Libbie, she looked like a page from *Delineator* altogether. She was wearing a sleeveless number from Monkey Ward's Better Frocks Department and long white gloves up to the armpit.

"Why, it's Morris!" said Libbie, jumping up as I walked in. "How good to see you, Morris," she said and gave me a kiss.

This confused me, I want to tell you. We're not known for kissing at my house. Sometimes after surgery, but that's about it.

"Morris," said Libbie, "may I present Jonathan Kaplan?"

Now I understood everything. This was the new guy Libbie met last week. Obviously things must have got serious already if Ma had the radio off and the brown silk on.

Jonathan Kaplan stood up and took my hand and gave me a smile, so I took his hand gave him a smile and we looked each other over for a minute. My policy is don't make up your mind too quick about people because it's awful easy to get fooled. Sometimes, for example, you meet a guy who looks as crooked as an alderman and he turns out to be dead honest. Or sometimes the other way around. So I held up judgment on Jonathan Kaplan. True, my first impulse when I saw him was to run quick and sew up my pockets, but what did that prove?

I snuck a quick glance at Ma and saw that she didn't

like the looks of Jonathan Kaplan also. She was glaring at him like he just offered her pickled pig's foot. But that didn't prove much either. The fact was that Ma hated everybody in the whole world unless they were on the radio.

So, as I say, I held up judgment on Jonathan Kaplan. All I did was shake his hand and say, "How do you do?"

"I don't do too great, Morris," he said. "Not tonight anyhow. Did you bring your billy club?"

"What billy club?" I said.

"I thought you might want to join in," he said. "Your mother is giving me the third degree."

"Yes, Mother, really!" said Libbie.

"Shut up and go make the little things," said Ma.

"The hors d'oeuvres?" said Libbie. "Of course, Mother."
She went into the kitchen.

"Sit down, Kaplan," said Ma. "You too, Morris."
We sat.

"To put you in the picture, Morris," said Jonathan Kaplan to me, "so far I've told your mother I'm from Cleveland, I came to St. Paul to start a new business, and I intend to marry Libbie."

"Did she believe any of it?" I said.

"Not yet," he said. "Do you?"

"Hell, no," I said.

"You will," he said. "Next question, Mrs. Katz."

"How old are you?" said Ma.

"How old is Libbie?" he said.

"Nineteen," said Ma.

"In that case I'm twenty-one," he said.

"I'd hate to hang since you were thirty-five," said

Ma but she had to grin for a second. She wasn't having too bad a time with Jonathan. It wasn't often anybody was brave enough to give her a workout.

"You still got family in Cleveland?" Ma said.

"Unfortunately no," said Jonathan. "My mother and father are both dead."

"From what?" said Ma. "Bullets?"

"Mrs. Katz," said Jonathan, "if you're so sure I'm a crook, tell me this: what have you got to steal?"

"Nothing," said Ma.

"Aha," said Jonathan.

"Never mind aha," said Ma. "You're after something, Kaplan. What?"

"Could you call me Jonathan?" said Jonathan.

"Never," said Ma. "Answer the question."

"What am I after?" said Jonathan. "To marry Libbie, of course."

"For what?" said Ma.

"For love," said Jonathan.

"You know something, Ma?" I said. "It's just crazy enough to be true."

"*Love?*" said Ma.

"Love," said I. "Believe me, it's a mysterious business, love."

"What do *you* know?" said Ma.

"Nothing," said I.

"That's right," said Ma, and turned to Jonathan. "Come on, Kaplan, what do you want from me?"

"Your mazeltov, that's all," said Jonathan. "So how's about it?"

"Not so fast, Baron Munchausen," said Ma. "One

thing you got to satisfy me first, and don't get cute. If you marry Libbie, which maybe I'll say yes and maybe not, how you gonna support her?"

"No problem," said Jonathan, and reached in his pocket and pulled out about three feet of red rubber tubing, a quarter inch in diameter. "Believe it or not, this is what I make my living with," he said. "Can you figure out how?"

"Well," said Ma, "it got to be one of two things: either you siphon gas or you give enemas."

"Wrong," said Jonathan. He leaned forward and lowered his voice. "I must ask you never to repeat what I'm gonna tell you," he said. "That's what happened in Cleveland. I had a real nice business going but too many people found out and that was the end. So far in St. Paul nobody knows but me. Please, I'm trusting you."

"So trust already," said Ma.

"Listen," said Jonathan. "There's over two hundred beer joints in St. Paul that serve beer on draft. Now, how do you chill draft beer? Here's how: between the keg and the tap there's a narrow coil that the beer runs through and that's what makes it cold. Okay? So by the end of the week this coil gets pretty well sludged up naturally and it got to be cleaned out. So what most beer joint owners do on Sunday morning when the joint is closed, they come down and take their taps apart and wash out the coil, a messy job nobody likes. So here's where I come in."

"Where?" said Ma.

"Just listen," said Jonathan. "A pal of mine back in Cleveland who's in the bar supply game showed me a little trick a few years ago. You don't need to take the whole tap apart to clean the coil. You just loosen the bottom of the coil and stick this tube on"—he held up one end of his little rubber tube—"and you blow"—he stuck the other end of the tube in his mouth and blew—"and in a couple seconds you got all the sludge blown out and the coil is clean like brand-new."

"So this is your professon?" said Ma. "Blowing dreck from beer coils?"

"Don't knock it," said Jonathan. "Every Sunday I go out and make the rounds of the beer joints. I don't charge much—two bits apiece, four bits if I can get it. For a price like that the boss is tickled to death to give me the job. And for me it's a breeze: one-two-three, blow, and good-by. I can cover a hundred places in a day. So for one easy day's work I bring home twenty-five, thirty, maybe forty bucks."

Suddenly a strange voice spoke up which we couldn't figure out for a second, then we looked over and saw it was Pa talking. "Pearl," he said to Ma, "this is a wonderful man. What you got against him?"

"Shut up. I'm thinking," said Ma. She sat and drummed her fingers on the table, never taking her beady eyes off Jonathan. I got to say it didn't bother him. He just sat with a cool grin and looked right back at her. Once he even tipped her a wink.

"*Foie gras*, anyone?" said Libbie, coming out of the kitchen with a plate of chopped liver on Triscuits.

"Libbie," said Jonathan, "Mother Katz has something to tell you."

"Who?" said Libbie.

"Nu?" said Jonathan, grinning at Ma.

"Momser," said Ma, "what kind of hipky-dripky are you making?"

"A fine way to talk to a son-in-law," said Jonathan.

"What?" hollered Libbie, getting frantic. "What? What? What?"

"Libbie, give me the liver you shouldn't drop it," said Ma.

"What?" Libbie kept hollering. "What?"

Ma took the liver. "Mazeltov, dearie," she said to Libbie.

Well of course it took twenty minutes to make Libbie stop crying, and then Ma sent Pa out to get a bottle of cream soda to celebrate. But Jonathan said never mind the cream soda. He came prepared with a bottle of champagne in his overcoat pocket. So he went and got it— imported French champagne. Even Ma said, "Hoo-ha!"

Oh, he was a lulu, that Jonathan Kaplan. You'd have thought the whole Orpheum circuit was in our living room. First he popped open the champagne and made a bunch of funny toasts. Then he sang "Cuban Pete" and danced the rhumba with Libbie and then he sang "Ut a Zoy" and danced the kazatsky with Ma. Then he did card tricks, bird calls, and imitations of Kay Kyser and Warner Oland, and for the grand finale he gave a demonstration of graphology, which is telling a person's character from their handwriting. He had us all write our signatures on a piece of paper (except Ma naturally who said she couldn't find her glasses but the truth is she can't write just like she can't read). By looking at our signatures Jonathan told us what kind of personalities we had, which he insisted was a real science and not a parlor trick, but I say bullshit. Anyone who looks at a signature and says it shows strength, wit, and ambition, and the signature is my father's, is not practicing any science I ever heard of.

But what the hell, Pa hadn't been so happy since his last pay check, and Libbie practically came unglued between laughing and crying, and Ma went the whole night without giving one single whammy to anybody. And me—well, of course I could see by this time that Jonathan was some kind of an arch-criminal and I knew that somehow he was going to give us all a terrible hosing, especially Libbie, but just the same I hollered and enjoyed and kept hoping the party would never end.

So I wasn't too pleased when all of a sudden my cousin Albert came busting in with his face all black and scowly. He headed right for me, but Libbie got to him first. "Albert darling," she said and kissed him. That stopped him, you can bet. "Albert," she said, "may I present Jonathan Kaplan, my fiancé?"

"What are you giving me?" said Albert.

"No, honest," said Libbie.

"True, Aunt Pearl?" said Albert, looking at Ma.

She shrugged.

"I'll be a sonofabitch," said Albert, shaking his head.

"Thank you for your kind wishes," said Jonathan, and took Albert's hand.

"Don't I know you from someplace?" said Albert.

"Maybe you saw his picture in the post office," said Ma.

"Write your name, Albert," said Libbie. "Jonathan will analyze your character."

"I got no time to bullshit," said Albert. "Morris, come outside."

He grabbed a hold of me so naturally I came outside.

"So how do you like my new brother-in-law-to-be?" I said.

"Shut up," said Albert. "Don't change the subject."

"You didn't give me the subject yet," I said.

"Bruce Albright called," said Albert.

"Maybe he should get a headset," I said. "He spends so much time on the phone. What did he say?"

"I said I was gonna break your jaw for you," said Bruce Albright, getting out of Albert's Maytag, all six feet four of him.

"But I talked him out of it," said Albert.

"Temporarily," said Bruce.

"I told him you'd give him your word never to see this Bridget cooz again," said Albert. "Would you do that, Morris?"

"Absolutely," I said. "A couple more weeks and she's all yours, Bruce."

"A couple more *weeks?*" Albert hollered.

"That does it," said Bruce. "Morris, put up your dukes."

"No, Bruce," said Albert. "I agree he got it coming, that schmuck, but all the same I can't let you do it."

"Butt out, Albert," said Bruce.

"No, Bruce," said Albert. "Believe me, I hate him worse than you do, but family is family."

"Albert, get out of my way," said Bruce. "Or are you looking for a broken jaw too?"

"Not especially," said Albert. "But if you want Morris you're gonna have to fight me first."

"Suits me," said Bruce and they squared off.

To tell you the truth it wasn't much of a fight. Albert, if you remember, was five feet one and Bruce was six feet four, so only one punch got thrown. Albert gave Bruce a shot in the balls and that was that.

"Well, Albert," I said after Bruce hobbled away clutching his parts, "I certainly appreciate this and if you ever need a favor, don't hesitate."

"I hope I never need nothing from you, you selfish, inconsiderate schmuck," said Albert.

"What do you mean?" I said.

"I mean those people in there," he said, pointing at my house. "Your family, Morris, your flesh and blood. Did you think about *them* when you started up with this Bridget cooz?"

"Well, not too much," I said, getting ashamed.

"Oh, Morris, Morris," he hollered, grabbing my hands, "are you gonna pull the chain on your own mother? And your father, that poor horse's ass? And how about Libble, especially now she's gonna marry that vagrant? What happens to all of them if you blow the Zimmerman money?"

I gave a big sigh. He was right, of course. I'd been kidding myself about Bridget, I saw that now. I couldn't keep her, not even temporary, not unless I wanted to risk losing Celeste and putting my whole family on the county. "Albert," I said, "you're right. I've been a schmuck. Tell me what to do."

"You've been a schmuck with earlaps," he said. "So listen carefully."

"All right," I said.

"Dump this Bridget cooz," he said. "Right now. To-night. Call her and give her the walking papers."

"It's eleven o'clock," I said. "They won't ring anyone in the dorm at this hour."

"So leave a message," said Albert. "That's better yet. You won't have to talk to her."

"All right," I said.

"Morris," he said, giving me a little squeeze on my shoulder, not too painful, "I know you feel crappy now. But think of all the great pussy you can buy after you marry the Zimmerman money."

Then he got in his Maytag and drove away and I went back into the house. Jonathan Kaplan was playing "Nola" with a spoon on six glasses of water and I sat down and listened to a few choruses but I wasn't really concentrating. Instead I was trying to think of a message to leave for Bridget at the women's dorm. I hated to say anything mean to her, but just the same it had to be strong enough so she'd know where she stood. I picked up a pencil and a piece of paper left over from the graphology demonstration and tried a few different combinations. Finally I got one that seemed about right:

> Dear Bridget,
>   It is best to break clean. I love another.
> Better luck next time.
>
> > Sincerely,
> > Morris Katz

I got up quietly, went into the kitchen where the phone was, and called the women's dorm.

"Women's dorm," said the operator.

"Hello," I said. "I would like to leave a message for Miss Bridget O'Flynn."

"Your name?" said the operator.

"Morris Katz," I said.

"The message?" said the operator.

I looked at the slip of paper in my hand. Then I looked at it some more.

"Hello," said the operator. "What is the message, please?"

" 'I love you,' " I said.

Chapter Seven

Okay, so I couldn't do it. Dump Bridget, I mean. Call me anything you want. I couldn't leave loose of the woman I loved, and that was that.

And naturally I couldn't dump Celeste either, not with all that Zimmerman gold. So I thought long and hard and here's the solution I came up with: since I couldn't dump either one, I would just have to hang on to both.

(Nu, how do you like that for clear thinking? You still got doubts that love can turn a rational human being into a blue-ass baboon?)

So anyhow I went to Celeste the next day and told her I had to be back on my night watchman's job at the First National Bank tonight and could I borrow her car again.

"Oh, poop on you," she said.

But I argued for a couple hours and promised I would take her out tomorrow night for sure and finally I wore her down. So at 7 P.M. I picked up Bridget at the women's dorm.

"Oh, Morris, Morris, Morris, Morris," said Bridget and took my arm and looked at me with her eyes all big and melty.

"Well, I guess you got my message," I said.

"Oh, Morris, Morris," she said again and kept on saying it and rubbing her face against my sleeve all the way to the River Bank.

I parked and held her gently and sniffed her hair and it was just like last night—great.

"Sweet eaglet," she said. "Gentle knight." She took my hand and pressed it against her cheek.

I liked that fine.

"Can it really be true?" she said. "That I am loved by a poet?"

"You're darn tootin'," I said.

"But not just any poet," she said. "A *Jewish* poet!"

"You deserve it, kiddo," I said.

"I shall try to deserve it, Morris," she said. "I shall try to please and comfort you in every way."

"You're off to a swell start," I said.

"I'll be your woman, yes, but I want to be your companion too," she said. "I want to go with you to concerts and museums and all the things you love."

"That's wonderful," I said, giving her a look. By me concerts and museums are right up there with root canal.

"And if you like," said Bridget, "I'll come along to your cell meetings too."

"What cell?" I said.

"The Communist Party, of course," she said.

"Hey, watch it!" I hollered, rolling up the window fast.

"It's all right, Morris," she said. "I *approve*, don't you see? In fact I *applaud*. If you Jews weren't in the vanguard, where would social progress be?"

"That's right," I said, wondering who put such bees

in her bonnet. Me a Communist? For Christ sakes, if I had eight dollars I'd have been a Republican.

"Well, Bridget," I said, "I'd certainly like to take you to my cell meetings, but it's members only."

"Couldn't I join?" she said.

"Not *my* cell," I said. "It's stag."

"Oh," she said.

"Slide over a little closer," I said.

"Don't you want to show it to me first?" she said.

"Show what to you?" I said.

"Your new poem," she said. "You said you'd bring it tonight."

"Which I meant to," I said. "But the thing is, I haven't been able to finish it. If you ask me, I think I'm having a little writer's block."

"Oh, my poor eaglet," she said. "What can I do to help?"

"You can slide over a little closer," I said.

"Yes, brave minstrel," she said and she slid over a little closer and I put my arm around her, just gently, and I sniffed her hair a few more times and that's how we sat, quiet and still. It was terrific, I'm not kidding. I never had such peacefulness in my life. Somehow I just couldn't worry about all the things I should have, like (a) I was in love with a shicksa who (b) was not only a shicksa but an Irish Catholic shicksa raised by nuns yet and who (c) had no money and was (d) also a little strange in the head: I mean what else do you call somebody who was convinced that all Jews were either listening to Beethoven or throwing bombs?

But as I say, I just couldn't be bothered with such

details right now. I was just too happy holding Bridget and sniffing her hair.

Bridget was happy also, generally speaking, although I think she'd have been happier if I'd done a little intercourse on her. I'm sure of it, in fact. But somehow I didn't feel like it tonight. Or let me put it another way: I *did* feel like it tonight. But it seemed to me the conditions were just about one hundred per cent wrong. After all, I wasn't sitting here with just a piece of ass; this was the woman I loved sweetly and tenderly and with all my heart. To take such a person and ram it into her in a parked car, do you call that nice? No, with such a person it ought to be something special—a field of daisies maybe, or a mountaintop would be good. But not here and not yet.

So whenever Bridget started in grinding and pumping and hollering, "Take me, eaglet!" I would just peel her off politely and give her a few pats to quieten her down. Then I'd go back to smelling her hair, which might not sound like such a big deal to you, but to me it was one of the truly outstanding nights of my entire life.

Well, the next night was not. I took out Celeste like I promised and it was lousy. But I'll be fair: for Celeste it was even lousier.

The trouble was I couldn't get it up. Who knows why? Something to do with loving Bridget maybe. All I can tell you is it came as one hell of a shock. Nothing like this had ever happened to me before, not once. "Everready Morris," they used to call me on Selby Avenue because I never failed with *anybody* and believe me, some of them were ugly enough for a circus. Most, maybe.

But tonight it just wouldn't work, no matter what. Celeste got crabby as hell of course. "A fine romance, my friend, this is!" she said, and gave me a kick.

"Look, these things happen," I said. "Ask your father."

"Well, it better not happen tomorrow night," she said.

"I got to work at the bank tomorrow night," I said.

Well, naturally Celeste threw six fits, but I held firm because this was my plan: alternate nights for each broad. I don't know if anybody ever had a worse plan. I doubt it.

With Celeste things kept getting tenser and tenser. True, I *did* manage to get it up the next time I took her out, but the time after that, again it was nothing doing. That's how it went: some nights I could, some nights no. The hell of it was I never knew in advance. And another problem came up: Celeste got so nervous worrying whether I could or couldn't, that sometimes when *I* could *she* couldn't. It was bad, I tell you, and I knew something had to snap soon.

Meanwhile with Bridget I could also feel trouble closing in. First of all, she kept shlepping me to the museum and the concert hall and naturally I had to keep pretending I was practically soiling my trousers from pleasure. I'd bat my eyes and suck in my breath and clap louder than everybody in the whole place put together. Not at the museum though; I learned that quick: don't clap in museums. I'm talking about concerts. At one concert, in fact, I clapped so loud that the bald-headed Greek who led the band came back and did four encores that nobody wanted. For a while there I thought the audience might lynch me.

But that wasn't the main trouble, the concerts and the museum. I still didn't have a poem; that was the main trouble. My cousin Crip was still laying in the Mayo Clinic and the weeks kept rolling by and nobody knew for sure when he was coming back including my Aunt Ida. So every time I saw Bridget I had to dream up some new excuse, and every time she believed me less.

Finally one night—Crip had been gone nearly a month by now—I walked into the women's dorm to pick up Bridget and there she stood in the lobby with her arms folded and her face like stone and I knew my time had come.

"Hi, there," I said.

"Bruce Albright has been phoning me," said Bridget.

"Don't listen to him," I said. "He is insane from jealousy and a painful crotch injury."

"He says you're a big liar and you couldn't write a poem to save your life," said Bridget.

"See? Nutty as a fruitcake," I said. "If I was you, I'd get a new phone number."

"Morris," she said, "when *exactly* am I going to have your poem?"

"Bridget," I said, "with poems you can't guarantee a delivery date. It's not like I was making you a potholder."

"Morris," she said, "I am not going out with you tonight."

"Why are you listening to crazy Bruce?" I said. "Listen to me who loves you."

"And I love *you*, Morris," she said. "Perhaps too much already. That is why I cannot risk more. I will not see you again until you bring me a poem. No, Morris, don't argue. My mind is made up."

I could see that it was. I could also see where I'd made my mistake: I should have boffed Bridget a long time ago and not waited around for fields of daisies. I'd have had her eating out of my hand by now, not asking tough questions. Well, what was done was done and there was no way to change it now, especially with the house mother watching.

So what next? Well, that was obvious: a trip to Rochester. No more waiting for Crip to get home; I had to go and see him. Of course Rochester wasn't exactly a streetcar ride; it was a good seventy-five miles away. Still, it wouldn't be too tough to make it back and forth in one day, especially in a new Olds.

So on Sunday, which I figured was the best day to con Celeste out of her car, I went over to her house about ten in the morning. The second I got there I saw something strange was going on. First of all, I heard this crazy noise, loud and shrill like a factory whistle, coming from inside the house. Second, Celeste's car was parked in the driveway with all four doors wide open and inside the car was A. M. Zimmerman behaving like a lunatic. His hair was wild and his eyes were popping and he was punching and poking into every corner of the car, jabbing the upholstery, yanking out the seats, lifting up the floor boards, digging in the glove compartment, the ashtrays, the side pockets.

"Good morning, Mr. Zimmerman," I said.

"I'll give you good morning, you bullshitter," he hollered. "Night watchman, huh? I checked with the First National."

"Oh-oh," I said.

"You got another broad, you cockaroach," he hollered. "And you're shtooping her in *my* car!"

"Honest I'm not," I said. "I swear on my mother."

"Bullshit," he said, and went back to searching the car.

"Is that Celeste I hear screaming?" I said because the noise was still going on, getting louder in fact.

"Aha!" hollered Mr. Zimmerman, holding up something he found in the corner of the seat—a gold cross on a thin gold chain which I suddenly remembered Bridget had been wearing around her neck one night. "All right, fuzzynuts," he said to me, "how did this get here?"

"Say, I bet I know how," I said. "I saw this elderly nun hitchhiking the other night so naturally I gave her a lift. Sister Mary Frances, her name was."

"Celeste!" he hollered, running up on the porch with the gold cross. "Look!"

Celeste and her mother came out on the porch. They were both of them crying which accounted for the volume.

"Good morning, Mrs. Zimmerman and Celeste," I said.

"See?" said Mr. Zimmerman, holding up the cross in front of Celeste.

She flang up her hands and shrank back like Count Dracula altogether.

"Now will you get rid of this low-life?" said Mr. Zimmerman to Celeste.

"Oh, why didn't I listen to my parents who gave me birth?" hollered Celeste.

"Can't we sit down and discuss this in a civilized manner over brunch?" I said.

"Get out out of here, you cockaroach, and don't ever come back," said Mr. Zimmerman to me.

I left with what you'd call mingled emotions. First I felt good and then I felt bad. What made me feel good was losing Celeste. What made me feel bad was I had to get her back.

Still I wasn't too worried at this point. I figured I'd ask Crip for *two* poems instead of one when I got to Rochester, one poem to re-hook each broad. Of course that would put me right back up the same crick—stuck with two broads and not able to dump either one—but that was something to worry about later.

Right now the problem was getting to Rochester. Naturally Celeste's car was out. And so was Albert's. Since he found out I was still hanging on to Bridget, he hadn't even talked to me, that's how mad he was. So I got out on the highway and started thumbing.

It's never much trouble hitchhiking to Rochester because there's always someone heading down there who's so sick he's happy to have an extra driver along in case he topples over in a coma. Sure enough I got picked up within five minutes by an old guy with a colostomy pouch. He stopped about a hundred times to empty it behind Burma Shave signs, but even so we made it easy by noon.

So I went and found Crip's room and I got to tell you it was the biggest shock of my life when I walked in. Now, I had seen Crip in a lots of different casts before, big ones and little ones, regular-shaped casts for legs and arms, custom jobs for clavicles and cheekbones, all varieties and sizes. But I never saw anything like the one I saw this time. It didn't even look like a cast; it looked like an Egyptian mummy. My entire cousin was in plaster from the head down—shoulders, arms, torso, legs, feet, toes—everything in one long continuous plaster mummy case.

"Well, Crip," I said, "I sincerely hope this treatment turns out to be a total and complete success."

"Thanks, Morris," he said.

"Because if it don't," I said, "they're gonna find two dead doctors at the bottom of the Rochester reservoir."

"Thanks," he said again. "So how's things at home?"

"That's why I came," I said. "There's kind of an emergency."

"Gee, I hope you don't need a poem," he said.

"As a matter of fact, I need two," I said.

"Oh, Morris, I'm so sorry," he said. "But as you see, I can't use my hands so how can I write?"

"What's the problem?" I said. "You dictate and I'll take it down."

"That's no good," he said. "My Muse don't work unless I can actually write the words on paper."

"What the hell kind of a Muse is that?" I said.

"I'm afraid you got to take the one they give you," he said.

"How long you got to be in this cast?" I said.

"The doctors are pretty vague," he said. "My guess is another month or two."

"Tell you what," I said. "I'll go get a tire iron and pry your hands loose. Wait right here."

"No, Morris," he said. "The whole idea is total immobility. The least little movement and I got to start all over."

"Well, we can't have that," I said. "So here's what we'll do. Since you can't dictate any *new* poems, dictate some of your *old* ones. That'll do just as good."

"I'm sorry, Morris, but they don't stay in my mind once they're written," he said. "All I can remember is the most recent."

"What's that?" I said.

"*To Celeste*," he said.

"Rats," I said because now I could see clearly what my situation was. Hopeless, that's what.

"I'm sorry, Morris," Crip said again. "Honest."

"Not your fault," I said, and gave him a pat on the cast. "Well, I'll be going. Stay loose, Crip."

So I left Mayo and thumbed a ride home. This time I got picked up by a guy with cataracts on both eyes. I asked several times if he wanted me to drive, but he didn't answer because he was deaf too. So I just settled back in the seat and relaxed, figuring maybe this was the best solution after all—a quick death on the Rochester–St. Paul highway.

But this wasn't my day; we got back safe.

Chapter Eight

Wait: it gets grimmer.

When I came home that night the house was full of people. What happened was Libbie had been hocking Ma every day to have a reception for Jonathan Kaplan but Ma had been saying no, hoping Jonathan would disappear. But he didn't, so finally Ma broke down and invited my uncles and aunts over to meet the groom.

I'll tell you about my uncles and aunts. My uncles were even more unemployed than my father, which you'll understand in a minute. The oldest, Uncle Benny, was a florist, a profession the 1936 labor market needed almost as bad as buffalo skinners. And here's something else about Benny. This was a man who suffered from terrible hay fever, so he went and picked the floristry business to go into. And what's more, he went and picked St. Paul, the hailstorm capital of the world, to put up a greenhouse. That's the kind of thinkers I had for uncles.

Uncle Shimen, the next oldest, was Crip's father. He was a piano tuner, which is right behind florist on the list of essential occupations. I don't think Shimen netted fifty dollars in a good year, and Aunt Ida pissed it all away on fruit.

The next oldest, Uncle Herschel, was the hardest of

all to believe. He was a *spats-maker,* for Christ sakes! I'm not kidding; he really was. I bet the last time Herschel saw a customer was under Coolidge.

The only uncle who might have made it except he had this fatal flaw in his character was the youngest, Uncle Labe. He was my cousin Albert's father but you never would have guessed it. Albert, as you know, was rougher than a cob, but Labe had a heart made out of pure mush and that's what ruined him. He was a credit dentist which is not a bad business at all but, believe me, you got to be ruthless. The minute a customer misses a payment, don't hesitate. Grab the dentures right out of their mouth, at mealtime if possible, otherwise they walk all over you. But Labe could never bring himself to do it so of course the word got around to every rotten-toothed deadbeat in town. Pretty soon all Labe had was accounts receivable and they came and took away the chair, the drill, the sink, and everything.

Well, you can see my uncles weren't exactly the Four Horsemen of Notre Dame. But my aunts were something else again. There were four of them too—Lena, Ida, Bryna, and Esther—and they were pisscutters, take my word. Maybe they weren't in a class with my mother, but they weren't too far behind. Everybody on Selby Avenue was scared of them, including butchers and landlords, even though they were little teensy women, none of them much bigger than a ferret. And what's more, they were all in terrible health. Every one had diabetes at least and most had a fallen womb. The sickest, I guess, was Aunt Bryna, Herschel's wife. In addition to all the regular sicknesses, she had a goiter and high blood pressure too.

For one condition she had to have salt every day, and for the other she dassn't, so she was always swoll up at one end or the other.

But sick and sawed-off as they were, these old broads were dynamite. Whatever little money came into their house, they went out and made. There was nothing they wouldn't hustle. They did dressmaking, baked strudel for bar mitzvahs, cooked moonshine, cut lawns, toilet-trained babies, cured sties, flicked chickens on Friday, hawked chrysanthemums outside the football stadium on Saturday, and parked cars in the St. Paul Auditorium Garage on fight nights and, mind you, not a one of them could drive.

So this was the gathering at my house that night. Actually there were *two* gatherings: the uncles were gathered around Jonathan on one side of the room, and the aunts were gathered around Ma on the other. Naturally all of them had come over, both the uncles and the aunts, thinking Jonathan must be some kind of a stiff if Libbie hooked him, but Jonathan charmed the ass off the uncles in no time at all, especially after he started analyzing their handwriting and telling them they were bold, resourceful, dynamic, and creative. So the uncles, and my father too of course, were all huddled around Jonathan laughing and applauding like a regular fan club. But the aunts, just like Ma, were immune to Jonathan's tricks. They didn't even crack a smile at his gags and as for his graphology, that was a total bust because they didn't know how to write any more than Ma did. So they all sat across the room, glaring at Jonathan, shaking their heads, and giving Ma sympathetic pats. And in between was Libbie, running back and forth in the white gloves kissing everybody nervously and passing a tray of Velveeta on Ritz Crackers.

"Well, Pearl," Aunt Lena said to Ma—Aunt Lena was Albert's mother, the former owner of the famous fur coat —"Well, Pearl," she said, "look at the bright side. At least Libbie ain't gonna be a old maid like everybody said."

"And at least he's Jewish," said Aunt Bryna. "Even a liar wouldn't lie about that."

"So you'll make a nice little wedding at home," said Aunt Ida. "How much could it cost?"

Then Ma dropped the bombshell. "No," she said, "the wedding ain't gonna be at home. The wedding is gonna be by the Lowry Hotel in the Grand Ballroom."

"*What?*" hollered everybody including Libbie and me.

"You heard me," said Ma. Her jaw was sticking out which meant her mind was made up and there was no chance in the world to change it. "By the Lowry Hotel in the Grand Ballroom," she said. "With flowers, a ice sculpture, and music by Ralph Rifkin and his Rhythm Ramblers."

"Oh, Mother!" Libbie hollered. "For *me?*"

"For *you?*" said Ma, giving Libbie a look. "You crazy or what?"

"For who then?" said Libbie.

"For the boychik," said Ma, turning to me.

"I don't understand," I said.

"Of course you don't understand," said Ma. "That's why you got a mother. So listen. This Kaplan I want in my house like I want mice. But as long as it's gonna happen, let's get some benefit."

"How?" I said.

"I'm inviting A. M. Zimmerman to the wedding," said Ma.

I gave a gasp.

"You think he won't come?" said Ma. "Don't worry, he'll come. You know why? Because Celeste Zimmerman is gonna be maid of honor."

"But, Mother," said Libbie, "I've already asked my oldest and dearest friend Ruthie Baumgarten."

"Shut up, I'm talking," said Ma. "Celeste is maid of honor in a pink taffeta formal which I will make her myself. And you, my boychik"—she gave my cheek a pinch—"are best man in a tuxedo altogether. And there you'll be under the chupah, Celeste in the pink formal and you in the tuxedo, by the Lowry Hotel in the Grand Ballroom with the flowers and Ralph Rifkin and his Rhythm Ramblers and I guarantee you, sonny, when A. M. Zimmerman sees what kind of classy people we are, he ain't gonna stand in your way no more."

"She's right, your Ma," said Aunt Esther. "If there's one thing that shtoonk Zimmerman respects, it's class."

"Naturally," said Aunt Lena. "Look what kind of a classy family he comes from. His father stole clothes from clotheslines and his mother went in the cellar with the landlord."

"But this will cost a fortune," I said.

"Worth it, dolly," said Aunt Ida. "If you ain't got the father on your side, you'll never get the daughter, I don't care if you're yentzing her six times a day."

"Ma," I said, "where's all this money coming from?"

"Don't worry, I took care," said Ma. "I went today by the loan shark and hocked everything I got in the world. What's the matter, sonny? Why are you sweating?"

"Nothing," I said. "It's hot in here."

"How could it be hot?" said Ma. "I used the coal money to make a deposit on the hotel. Morris, is everything okay by you and Celeste?"

"Of course," I said. "So when's the wedding?"

"Three weeks from Sunday," said Ma.

I felt the blood run out of my head. "So soon?" I said.

"With a gypsy like Kaplan you don't waste time," said Ma. "Morris, you look funny. You *sure* everything's okay by you and Celeste?"

"Couldn't be better," I said, trying to put on a smile, but Ma kept giving me a look, so I figured the best thing for me was to get the hell out of there.

So I went and took a slow walk down Selby Avenue, not going anywhere special, just shlepping along and wondering how soon the next disaster was going to hit me. It wasn't long. As I went past the Sel-Dale Bar and Grille, Rummy Rosenberg, the only Jewish drunk in St. Paul and one of the few in the whole world, came out and puked on my suit.

Chapter Nine

When your luck goes, it goes, that's all.

The whole following week I kept trying to get to Celeste, but how could I when she never showed up at school? Naturally I tried calling her on the phone, but each time I did, the butler hung up on me. And I couldn't get to Bridget either. Every day I'd go to the *L'Etoile du Nord* and every day Lance Berman and Claude Applebaum would throw me out. And don't think they couldn't. They might have been fruits but there's no size limit on the breed and these two were as big as zeppelins.

Finally I got fed up one day. I grabbed their teapot in one hand and their picture of Hart Crane in the other and I told them either they let me in or I started smashing.

"But she has somebody with her," they said.

"Here goes Hart Crane," I said, and whammed it into the wall.

That did it. They bit their knuckles and got out of my way and I ran into Bridget's office hollering her name. But I stopped hollering as soon as I got through the door. Lance and Claude hadn't been lying; there *was* somebody with Bridget: a nun.

Now, I'm not a nut like my mother when it comes to

nuns. I mean I don't believe for one second they really
drink the blood of Jewish babies, not in the Twin Cities
anyhow, but all the same there's a lot of people I'd rather
bullshit with than nuns. Still, here was Bridget and that
was the main thing.

I could tell she was just as excited to see me as I was
to see her. Her eyes got all shiny and her mouth started
to smile and she jumped up like she wanted to run into
my arms. But only for a second. All of a sudden she sat
down and stopped smiling and didn't look at me.

"I assume you brought a poem," she said, real cold.

"As a matter of fact, no," I said. "But—"

"Then please leave, Morris," she said.

"Morris, is it?" said the nun. She was a little old freckle-
faced woman with glasses and a brogue. "Aha," she said,
"so you're the Hebrew who's got this child at sixes and
sevens. I'm Sister Mary Frances."

"How do you do?" I said. I looked for a ring to kiss but
she wasn't wearing any so I just kneeled for a couple
seconds.

"I like you Hebrews, Morris," said Sister Mary Frances.
"You're devious, of course, and scandalous cheats, and
there *is* the matter of killin' Christ. Still, what I always
say is any race that gave the world Heifetz and chicken
soup can't be all bad."

"I'll have my Ma make you a jar," I said.

"A big jar, mind, with matzo balls," said Sister Mary
Frances. "'Tis my passion, chicken soup, right after Christ
and poetry. And speakin' of which, are you a poet yourself or are you doin' the dirty to poor Bridget as I sus-
pect?"

"I'm a poet, I'm a poet," I hollered.

"Then why don't you write poems?" said Sister Mary Frances.

"Because I'm miserable, is why," I said. "Who can write poems if they're not happy?"

"'Tis true," said Sister Mary Frances. "Take that merry elf Edgar Allan Poe, for instance."

"Very funny," I said to Sister Mary Frances. "And you can forget the chicken soup."

"Morris," said Sister Mary Frances, "this child is sweeter than life to me. I'll not have you deceivin' her."

"I'm not," I hollered. "I swear to God."

"Careful, son," said Sister Mary Frances. "With me around it might be official."

I saw her point. Not that I believed in God too much. I mean I'm not like my mother who says, "If there's no God, go explain radio." But still and all, who knew for sure? So why take chances, especially the way my luck was running?

"On second thought I won't swear," I said. "You know why?"

"Yes," said Sister Mary Frances.

"No, you don't," I said. "I won't swear because the fact is I don't know any more if I can still write poetry. I might just be too crumpled up inside. Remember that, Bridget, the next time you decide to monkey around with a sensitive artist."

"Oh, Morris!" Bridget hollered, and looked at me like her heart was breaking. Mine was, I'll tell you that.

So I reached out my hand to Bridget and she reached hers back but before we could touch, Sister Mary Frances picked up a ruler and gave Bridget a whack across the knuckles. "Don't let this devil dazzle you, girl," she said. "Stick by your guns: a poem or nothin'."

"You're right of course, Sister," said Bridget.

"Why don't you go cure a leper?" I said to Sister Mary Frances.

"We'll give you till tomorrow to bring in a poem," said Sister Mary Frances.

"We?" I said. "I got to deal with *you* too?"

She gave a mean smile and nodded. "Good day, you sly semite," she said.

"Good day, yourself," I said, and went out to see if I could find someone to write me a poem in a hurry.

First I tried Henry Leibowitz. You remember Henry— the straight-A kid who rode to school with Albert and me and did our homework. "Henry," I said, "I'll give you a dollar cash if you write me a poem."

"That's a deal," he said. "And here's the poem:

> *Hot-cha*
> *Boop boop a doop.*
> *Mother's making*
> *Blubber soup.*"

"Cut the comedy," I said. "Don't you want the money?"

"Like life itself," he said. "But what makes you think I can write poems?"

"You get all A's, don't you?" I said.

"But that's *memory*," he said. "A whole nother thing. If you want, I'll *memorize* a poem for you, any poem you pick, I don't care how long. In fact, for a buck I'll give you *Evangeline* and throw in *The Rime of the Ancient Mariner.*"

"No, thanks," I said.

"Wait," he said. "Tell you what I'll do: *Evangeline* and *Ancient Mariner* plus *The Faerie Queene*, all eight cantos."

"So long, Henry," I said.

"For fifty cents?" he said.

But I just dragged myself away and went looking for somebody else to write me a poem. I looked and looked but it was impossible. Finally I decided the only solution was to try it myself. I don't mean *writing* a poem; I wasn't that crazy. I mean stealing a poem, which was also pretty crazy when you consider Bridget knew practically every poem ever written. Still, what choice did I have?

I tried to go about it as shrewd as possible. First, I looked through the back shelves of the library till I found books that were so covered with dust that I could tell nobody had taken them out for years. And second, I didn't steal any *one* poem. What I did was steal little dribs and drabs from *lots* of poems and string them together. So even if anybody recognized a part of my poem, they still wouldn't recognize the whole thing.

When I finished stitching up the poem I looked it over and to tell you the truth, it seemed pretty good to me. But it also seemed pretty bad too; that was the confusing part.

Not being too confident, I decided the best thing was to get an expert opinion before I sprung the poem on

Bridget. I went to Mr. Harwood's office. He wasn't exactly my favorite American, that prick, but poetry he knew, no question.

"Mr. Harwood," I said, "I wonder if you'd read this and tell me what you think."

"Certainly," he said. "A bit of baggy-pants salacity is always welcome in my bleak life."

I handed him the poem. "*Ode on Melancholy,*" he said. "Catchy title."

"You like it?" I said.

"Adore it," he said. "Do you mind if I read aloud?"

"Go ahead," I said, and he did:

ODE ON MELANCHOLY

If I should die think only this of me:
I loved not wisely but too well.
I thought thou wert a blessed damozel
But, nay, thou wert a belle dame sans merci.

Rememberest not, O mistress mine,
To err is human, to forgive divine?
Did He who made the lamb make thee?
So show a little charity.

Hey nonny, be not like a wolf on the fold,
For somewhere an angel with a book of gold
Is writing the names who love thee best
And, lo, Morris Katz leads all the rest!

Mr. Harwood put the poem down and took off his glasses and stared at me for a long time. "Mr. Katz," he said finally, "I have a grotesque feeling this is not a jape."

"What's a jape?" I said.

"I'm right," he said. "Dear God!"

"You don't care for the poem?" I said.

"Appalling," he said.

"That bad, huh?" I said.

"Execrable," he said. "Cretinous."

"Okay, I get the idea," I said.

"Did you write it yourself?" he said.

"Of course," I said.

"Did you write the last one too?" he said. "The one about Celeste?"

"Of course," I said.

"Did something happen to you between those two works?" he said. "Something that might result in brain damage?"

"You said it," I said.

"That could account for it," he said. "But I'm dubious. Something murky is going on. Would you care to tell me what?"

"No," I said.

"Good," he said. "If there's one thing I can't abide, it's the problems of undergraduates."

"You sure picked the right business," I said.

"No, Mr. Katz," he said, "the business I *picked* was to be a madly successful novelist. This is the business I *got*."

"There's worse things," I said. "Stop whining."

"You're right, of course," he said. "Rude, but right."

"Look who's talking about rude," I said. "Can I have my poem back?"

"With dispatch," he said. "What are you going to do with it?"

"Make a paper airplane," I said.

"A sound decision," he said.

But actually what I was going to do with the poem was give it to Celeste. Maybe it wasn't good enough for Bridget, but for Celeste it was plenty okay. The only problem was, where the hell was Celeste? She still hadn't showed up at school and the butler was still short-stopping my calls.

I tried once more, disguising my voice this time.

"Zimmerman residence," said the butler.

"May I talk to Miss Zimmerman?" I said.

"Who's calling, please?" said the butler.

"Professor Harwood," I said.

"Of course you may talk to Miss Zimmerman, sir," said the butler.

"Swell," I said.

"Appear in person at the front door," said the butler. "She will be happy to see you any time."

"Good day," I said.

"Good day, Mr. Katz," said the butler. "And if you're thinking of sending a letter, be advised that Miss Zimmerman's mail is being intercepted."

So I went home feeling like a dog's breakfast and believe me, what I saw at home didn't cheer me up any. Ma was still working on the plans for Libbie's wedding. Every day she added new names to the guest list—doctors, lawyers, accountants, insurance adjusters, tax appraisers, and anybody else who might give a little class to the affair. Most of them were practically strangers but that didn't matter; they got invited anyhow and the wedding kept growing bigger and bigger, fancier and fancier, more and more expensive, and all to impress A. M. Zimmerman who was never going to show up.

"So where's Celeste?" said Ma when I walked in. "How many times I told you bring her home so I can measure her for the pink taffeta formal?"

"She got homework," I told Ma. "I'll bring her tomorrow."

"That's what you said yesterday," said Ma, giving me a look. "Morris, you positive everything's okay by you and Celeste?"

"Absolutely," I said. "Believe me, Ma."

"I believe you, sonny," she said. "You know why?"

"Why?" I said.

"Because if you're lying I'm gonna put my head in the oven," said Ma.

Well, that settled that. I made up my mind right then and there I was going to see Celeste tonight even if I had to bust her door down. So I went to get Albert in case I did.

I'll tell you how things were between me and Albert. Things were okay again. Because in the last week Albert himself had had a tragedy of his own and he had learned, like I did, what it was to have your hopes in tatters and your dreams in ruins.

You remember what I told you about Albert's lousy luck with broads? To begin with he struck out with Miss Zucker, but at least he got to bang her maid. But after that there weren't even any consolation prizes, just blanks, one failure after another. Then suddenly his luck changed. He took out this Irene Farber, a fat broad in

Remedial English with bushy nostrils whose father owned the biggest work-gloves store in St. Paul, and sure enough he got in.

Well, Albert was flying high there for a while. But not long. Because a couple days later he found out something he didn't know: he had picked up the crabs from Miss Zucker's maid. And Irene Farber found out she had picked them up from Albert, and that was the end of that bonanza.

So now Albert also knew what disappointment was like, and it made him a kinder, humbler person and we were friends again. So on this night we're talking about I went to the Sel-Dale Rec and found Albert sitting there with his balls painted blue and I told him I needed to get to Celeste right away and would be help me. "Of course," he said, so we hopped in the Maytag and drove over to the Zimmerman house.

"I'll wait in the car," said Albert. "If they give you any trouble, holler."

"Okay," I said and started up the path to the house but before I was halfway there the front door opened and out came Celeste in a hat and coat with her mother and father and the butler. The butler was carrying a big trunk with Celeste's initials on it.

We all stopped dead when we saw each other, except for the butler. He kept on walking and put the trunk in the back of Celeste's Oldsmobile which was parked in the driveway. But I just stood still and gawked, Celeste stood still and blinked, Mr. Zimmerman stood still and ground his teeth, and Mrs. Zimmerman grabbed a hold of a tree and started bawling.

"Get out of here from here!" Mr. Zimmerman hollered at me.

"Celeste," I said, "where are you going?"

"Don't talk to me, you cockaroach," said Celeste.

"Celeste," I said, "you got to stop listening to your father. He has taken a strange dislike to me."

"So have I," said Celeste.

"You'll feel different after you read this," I said.

I tried to hand her my poem called *Ode on Melancholy* but Mr. Zimmerman jumped in front of her.

"Are you going?" Mr. Zimmerman said to me.

"Not till Celeste reads this," I said to Mr. Zimmerman.

"Sven," Mr. Zimmerman said to the butler, "knock him down."

"Yes, sir," said the butler, and started walking toward me.

"Albert!" I hollered.

Albert got out of his car. The butler took a look and stopped walking toward me.

"Sven, did you hear me?" said Mr. Zimmerman.

"*You* knock him down," said the butler to Mr. Zimmerman.

"You're fired," said Mr. Zimmerman. "Celeste, get in the car."

"Celeste, where are you going?" I said again.

"I'll tell you where she's going," said Mr. Zimmerman. "She is going to the Frances Shimer Junior College in Mount Carroll, Illinois. How do you like that, Mr. Emptypockets?"

"Wait!" I hollered to Celeste. "Read this first."

I tried to hand her the poem again but Mr. Zimmerman jumped in the way. "She ain't reading nothing," he said.

"All right, I'll read it out loud," I said.

"She got no time to listen," said Mr. Zimmerman.

"Yes, she has," said Albert and took the front seat out of the Olds.

So I read my poem out loud.

There was a silence afterwards and several people scratched their head.

"Well?" I said to Celeste.

"Sounds kind of familiar," she said.

"Of course it does," I said. "That's because it's what they call iambic. All your best love poems are."

"Oh," said Celeste.

"I think it's great in my opinion," said Albert.

"Really?" said Celeste. "What do you think, Sven?"

"A pastiche," said the butler. "Grossly derivative."

"See?" said Albert to Celeste.

"I hope you ain't expecting no references," said Mr. Zimmerman to the butler.

"So is it on again, you and me?" I said to Celeste.

"Never!" hollered Mr. Zimmerman.

"He's not talking to you," said Albert to Mr. Zimmerman.

"Well?" I said to Celeste.

"Give me the poem," she said.

I gave her the poem and she looked it over for a while. "Well," she said finally, "here's how I figure. No. 1: this was not my idea, going off to Frances Shimer Junior College. My stars, if I can't find a boy in a huge metropolitan center like the Twin Cities, what can I expect in

Mount Carroll, Illinois? . . . No. 2: I hate you, Morris Katz, you cockaroach, and I will never trust you again. But on the other hand it was you who first awakened me as a woman and that got to count for something . . . So No. 3: I can't see any reason not to start up with you again. Naturally I'll keep my eye out for something better, but meanwhile why not?"

"I'll tell you why not," hollered Mr. Zimmerman. "You're going to Frances Shimer Junior College, that's why not."

"I'll run away," said Celeste.

"I'll run away with you," I said.

"Armand," shrieked Mrs. Zimmerman to Mr. Zimmerman, "don't send her!"

"You tell him, lady," said Albert to Mrs. Zimmerman.

"Shit," said Mr. Zimmerman to everybody.

"I love you," I said to Celeste.

"In a pig's valise," said Celeste. "And let me tell you something else, you cockaroach. There's gonna be no more On-Again Off-Again Finnegan. From now on it's me every night and I don't mean maybe. You got that?"

"He got it," said Albert. "Ain't you, Morris?"

"I got it," I said, and Albert put the front seat back in the Olds. "So how's about it, Celeste?" I said. "Shall we go for a little spin?"

"I'll kill the both of you first!" hollered Mr. Zimmerman.

"Better wait till tomorrow," said Celeste to me.

"Maybe you're right," I said. "Well, good night, good night, parting is such sweet sorrow."

Then Albert and I got in the Maytag and drove

away giggling and hugging each other. I wish now I hadn't been in such a hurry to go. I wish I had stayed another couple seconds and told Celeste not to submit the new poem to the *L'Etoile du Nord.*

Chapter Ten

A week before the wedding Libbie said to me, "Morris, you know what would be charming?"

"No," I said.

"If you gave a bachelor dinner for Jonathan," she said.

"Who's gonna pay for it?" I said.

"I got ten dollars," she said. "Don't tell Ma."

Well, I wasn't exactly in a mood to throw a party. In fact, I was as low as a person gets. Things were worse than ever with Bridget thanks to that meatball Celeste who went and submitted my new poem to the *L'Etoile du Nord*. "Go," was all Bridget said to me after she read the poem, just "Go." I told her it was only a little jape because by now I'd looked up "jape" but that didn't help. "Go," was all she said. Even Sister Mary Frances was kinder than that; she offered to pray for me at least.

So you can see why I was in no mood for a party. But on the other hand a bachelor dinner for Jonathan would give me an excuse to get a night off from Celeste which believe me, I needed badly. Since we got back together again Miss Steamydrawers hadn't let loose of me for one second. So I told Libbie okay and started organizing the dinner.

I figured ten bucks would cover eats for ten people

with no trouble so that's how many I invited. Then I went around to a few restaurants to see where I could get the best deal. It narrowed down finally to Amendola's Little Napoli and the Shanghai Sanitary Pagoda. Little Napoli offered full-course dinners for ten including antipasto, minestrone, spaghetti and meatballs, gnocchi, spumoni, and two gallons of dago red. The Shanghai Sanitary offered egg rolls, fried shrimps, wonton soup, chicken chow mein, pork foo young, kumquats, fortune cookies, and all the tea we could drink. In terms of volume the chinks were better than Little Napoli but of course they didn't include wine.

So I asked Albert what he thought and he came up with a new idea altogether: why blow the money on food when for ten bucks we could all go to the whorehouse?

I hesitated. First off, I was in no desperate need to get my end wet, as you know. Second, I'm frankly not too big a fan of whorehouses; I prefer the thrill of the chase even if it means a bum lay and a steering wheel in the back. And third, I wasn't quite sure this was the right thing to do, getting my sister's fiancé laid, especially with her money.

"Why don't you leave it up to Jonathan?" said Albert. "It's his party."

So I did. I went to Jonathan, explained the choices, and asked him to decide.

"Well, Morris," said Jonathan, "let me put it this way. I never yet saw gnocchi that compared with nookie and I'd rather screw young than foo young. Does that answer your question?"

"Yes," I said and off we went to Cockeye Jennie's in

Minneapolis where for a dollar apiece you could pick from a nice selection of girls, all government inspected, ten minutes per trick, any style you like—regular, continental, or half-and-half.

It was a good value, no question, but the real attraction at Cockeye Jennie's wasn't the girls, it was the atmosphere. It was like a club, kind of. You'd wait downstairs in a big room full of comfortable chairs and the girls would keep walking through in their teddies, but not hustling you, just showing what they had. If you saw something you liked, you'd take her upstairs. If not, you'd just sit and bullshit with the guys as long as you wanted to. Jennie didn't believe in high pressure, that was the nice part.

Anyhow, the bunch of us walked in that night and sat down and as usual Jonathan started doing his stuff. First he sang, "Give me ten men who are stout hearted men," and then he told a couple hundred jokes and then he imitated a screech owl with the piles and then he analyzed everyone's handwriting including the whores.

Naturally he was a smash. For over an hour we all sat around plotzing from laughter, even Cockeye Jennie, but finally she got businesslike. "Gents," said Jennie, "there's no hurry of course but I'd like you to take a look at the newest member of our team." She pointed at a banjo-assed blond in green and gold teddies. "This gorgeous young thing just arrived from Chicago," said Jennie, "and you know what hot stuff they got in Chicago. Gents, say hello to Carla Sandburg."

"Hi, honey," said Jonathan. "Butchered any good hogs lately?"

"Oh, you!" said Carla.

"Okay, boys, who's for Carla?" said Jonathan.

"Me!" hollered Henry Leibowitz. "For God sakes, me!" Henry had never been to a whorehouse before—how could he with no money?—and he was so excited he'd already come several times. So he rushed upstairs with Carla and pretty soon the other guys started pairing off and disappearing until at last only Jonathan and me were left.

"You in a hurry to go upstairs?" I said to Jonathan.

"Not especially," he said. "Why?"

"I thought we might talk a little," I said. "I mean here we are practically brothers and what do I really know about you?"

"What's to know?" he said. "I'm a simple, honest businessman, that's all."

"Yeah, and I'm Sister Kenny," I said. "Come on, Jonathan, anybody can see you're a thief and a swindler. And that's what got me so puzzled. What the hell do you expect to get from us?"

"Affection and friendship, my boy," he said. "What else is there."

"Thank you and up your hoon," I said. "Listen, I know this is a lot to ask, but couldn't you tell the truth for just a little while?"

"How long?" he said.

"Ten seconds," I said. "All I want to know is this: what do you do? I mean *really*. Don't give me that crap about how you go out on Sunday morning and blow beer coils with your little red hose."

Jonathan made a sigh. "Well, Morris," he said, "I guess

I should have known I'd never put one over on a sharp operator like you."

"Damn right," I said.

"So I'm gonna tell you," he said. "But first you got to give me your solemn oath it goes no further."

"My hand to God," I said, raising it.

"Okay, here's what I do," he said and made his voice into a whisper. "I got a deal with all the circumcisionists in town. They save the foreskins they slice off during the week and I pick 'em on Sunday. A nickel a skin, I pay."

"What the hell do you do with foreskins?" I said.

"What do you think?" he said. "I ship 'em to Ireland, they plant 'em over there, and they grow up to be policemen."

Then he busted out laughing and threw his arms around me, mostly so I wouldn't be able to belt him, but in a second I was laughing myself and hugging him back. How do you stay sore at a barrel of monkeys like Jonathan?

"Jonathan, you slippery sonofabitch, I like you," I said which I did. "You're cunning as a shithouse rat and I wish to God you had your hooks in somebody else's sister, not mine, but still and all I never met anyone as peppy as you in my whole life and I got to admit it: I like you."

"I'm glad," he said. "Because I like you back, kid, and that's a fact."

"Thanks," I said.

"And listen," he said. "Don't worry about your sister."

"I won't," I said. "With Libbie what's the use worrying? You always know how it's gonna come out: bad. At least from you she'll get a few laughs along the way."

"I don't suppose I can convince you you're wrong," he said.

"No," I said.

"Then there's only one thing left to say," he said.

"What?" I said.

"Let's go upstairs and get banged," he said.

So we did and that was Jonathan's bachelor party.

Continuing the roundup of pre-wedding activities, I'll tell you now about the pink taffeta formal for Celeste.

It took a little doing to get Celeste over so Ma could fit her for that dress. The first time I asked her she said, "Go lay an egg. I don't even know your sister. What do I want to be her maid of honor for? And besides I think your mother is icky."

But gradually Celeste turned more agreeable. Here's why: her sex life was back to normal. That is, she was getting laid every night. True, there were still times when I couldn't get it up, but Jonathan, the old pussy-maven, taught me a trick which fixed that. He told me when your cock wouldn't cooperate, close your eyes and imagine the broad you're with is some glamorous movie queen you've always had the hots for.

Well, it worked but not quite the way Jonathan described. For instance, the first time I was in trouble I closed my eyes and tried to imagine Celeste was Ginger Rogers. But nothing happened except I felt like tap dancing. Next I ran through Dorothy Lamour, Madeleine Carroll, and Marlene Dietrich which you'll agree you can't do better, but still it just drooped. Then by luck I thought of a new twist. Instead of imagining that only

Celeste was a movie star, I imagined the *both* of us were. Like if she was Jeanette MacDonald, I was Nelson Eddy. If she was Ruby Keeler, I was Dick Powell. And that did it—or at least most of the time. Occasionally I found I needed still more help, so I'd expand a little—like I was John Garfield and Celeste was all four Lane sisters. That never failed.

Anyhow Celeste's disposition was a lot better lately— hers, not mine—so finally she broke down and came home with me to get fitted. Libbie and Ma and Pa were there and also Aunt Lena, Albert's mother, who was the best seamstress of all the aunts so she was going to help Ma with the sewing, seeing as how there wasn't a lot of time left before the wedding.

"Hello, dearie," Ma said to Celeste when I brought her in. Pa just nodded. He was sulking a little. It was Sunday but on account of Celeste's fitting, Pa's regular reading of Itzik Fishel's poem had been canceled. So he just nodded.

Then Libbie stepped forward with a big smile and a pair of white gloves so long she must have started putting them on the night before. "Ah," said Libbie, "this must be the famed Celeste about who I've heard such wonderful things."

"How do you do?" said Celeste.

"May I kiss you?" said Libbie. "I feel we're almost family in a matter of speaking."

"Well, okay," said Celeste, and Libbie kissed her.

"And this is my dear Aunt Lena," said Libbie.

"You don't want to kiss me, do you?" said Celeste to Lena.

"Feh," said Aunt Lena.

"How do you do?" said Celeste.

"How do you do?" said Aunt Lena.

"Would you care for some refreshments, my dear?" said Libbie to Celeste. "You'll find these biscuits rather delightful."

"No thanks," said Celeste. "I'm not too crazy about Oreos."

"Maybe she'd like a wiener," said Pa.

"Actually what I'd like is to get this over with," said Celeste.

"Who wouldn't?" said Ma. "Turn around a couple times, dearie."

So Celeste turned around a couple times while Ma and Aunt Lena looked her over.

"You sure you got enough material, Pearl?" said Aunt Lena.

"Six yards is not enough?" said Ma.

"I don't know," said Aunt Lena. "The tochess alone got to be four yards."

"But you'll save on top," said Ma. "There she got nothing."

"All right, but the skirt got to go all the way to the floor," said Aunt Lena. "Look at them legs, God forbid."

"Why, I think Celeste has a darling figure," said Libbie.

"Is there nothing but liars in this family?" said Celeste.

"Enough talking," said Ma. "Libbie, get the pins. Celeste, take off the clothes. Morris, Nathan, get out of the room."

"Don't go far, Morris," said Celeste.

"He won't," said Pa. "He'll be in the kitchen listening to Itzik Fishel."

So with Celeste's dress out of the way, we started looking for a tux for me. Naturally we weren't going to rent one if we could borrow one for free, so we called everybody we knew who owned a tux—two people altogether. Unfortunately they were the wrong size—too small, not too big. If they'd been too big the aunts would have cut the suits down in a minute. In fact, Aunt Esther suggested borrowing the two tuxes that were too small and stitching them together, but Ma suddenly came up with a better idea.

"You know who got a tux," she said.

"Who?" we said.

"I just told you," said Ma. "You-Know-Who."

"Ah," we said because now we understood. You-Know-Who was my officially dead cousin Seymour whose name you dassn't mention since he married the shicksa.

And it was true about Seymour having a tux. He bought one a few years back when he was working as a waiter in the Ryan Hotel dining room. In fact, that's where he met the famous shicksa. It was during State Fair week, I remember, and she had come down from Bemidji with her 4-H club. Hulda Asleksen, her name was, a blond girl with thighs like trees. Anyhow, Seymour was the waiter at her table and they got to kidding back and forth and he kept trying to make a date, which she was willing enough, but she had to be in bed by nine every night and he didn't finish work till ten. So finally they made a date for Seymour's night off.

The trouble was that on the afternoon of Seymour's night off, Hulda's calf, which had been a heavy favorite in the Guernsey judging at the State Fair, came in ninth in a field of nine. Who knows why? It's part of the game, that's all.

Hulda took it real hard. She managed to keep the date with Seymour all right, but the whole night long all she did was sit there and cry with those big round thighs. And there was Seymour, basically a soft-hearted person but also dying from a hard on. You know the rest: in order to stop the bawling and start the humping, he finally had to propose.

Well, it's happened to better guys than Seymour. Anyhow, he was living up in Bemidji now with Hulda where naturally who needs a tux? So it was still hanging in his former closet at home, and that's where Ma and I went to see if it would fit me. It was kind of a delicate subject because you could never mention Seymour's name, so Ma approached it very carefully.

Seymour's mother and father were my Aunt Bryna and Uncle Herschel (the spats-maker; you remember Herschel) so first Ma exchanged a little bullshit about this and that and then she finally popped the question. "Listen," she said, "you yourself don't have a son, everybody knows that. But if you did, what size would he be?"

"Thirty-six short," said Aunt Bryna.

"That's it," I said and we checked off the tux situation.

Next Ma went to hire a rabbi for the wedding. There were three synagogues in St. Paul but one was Reform so naturally to this one we didn't belong. The other two were Orthodox and at one time or another we'd been members of both.

First we belonged to the Sons of David but that ended when Ma got into a fight with the rabbi—Rabbi Greenberg, his name was. What happened was Ma was cleaning a chicken one day and she found a little piece of something hard in the gizzard. According to the rules, if there's anything in the gizzard that's made out of metal, the chicken is not kosher. But if it's made out of sand or gravel, the chicken *is* kosher. But you're not allowed to decide by yourself; you got to take the chicken to a rabbi.

So off Ma went to Rabbi Greenberg and he took a look at the gizzard and he said, "Too bad, missus. That's a cuff link."

"What are you talking?" Ma said. "That's a piece gravel."

"With *initials?*" said the rabbi.

So of course Ma did what everybody does in those cases: you eat the chicken and join a different shul.

So we joined the Sons of Zion, and in fact we were still members but Ma decided not to have the rabbi marry Libbie—Rabbi Sopkin, his name was. It wasn't that Ma didn't like Rabbi Sopkin; she did; everybody did. He was a nice easy-going old guy who was always willing to turn a blind eye when you showed up with a chicken who had metal in the gizzard, but the point was he *did* have a blind eye. He wore a black patch over it when he remembered but generally he forgot. Also he had this bad stammer and there was a hunch on his back, not too big, but you could notice it all right, don't worry. And another thing: I don't mean any disrespect, but facts are facts. Rabbi Sopkin was a terrible farter. And not little sneaky ones either; great big rolling ones, and steady. My Uncle Shimen, a veteran, said it reminded him of Château-Thierry.

Well, as I said, we all liked Rabbi Sopkin but here's how Ma figured and I think she was right: why spend a whole fortune to impress A. M. Zimmerman and then drag in a comedy rabbi to cock it up?

So Ma decided to call in Rabbi Pflaum of Temple Beth El which surprised hell out of me because Beth El was the Reform shul, and Ma has always had only one word for Reform Jews: *goyim.*

Still and all, if class was what Ma was after, she couldn't have done better than Rabbi Pflaum. Class he had plenty, right down to the white piping on his vest. And what a fancy talker! He talked even fancier than Mr. Harwood, that prick adviser of mine at the University. "Esteemed lady," Rabbi Pflaum said to Ma, "I shall be happy to officiate, for is not marriage an honorable estate?"

Ma just gave him a look; she didn't understand a word.

"What stipend have you in mind?" he said.

This she understood. "Five dollars," she said.

"Surely you jest," he said.

"Take it or leave it," Ma said.

"Come, madam, haggling is not seemly," he said. "I'll take twenty dollars."

"Six," said Ma.

"Fifteen," he said. "The ball is in your court."

"Seven-fifty," she said.

"Where will this wedding occur?" he said.

"By the Lowry Hotel in the Grand Ballroom," she said.

"All right," he said. "Ten dollars plus supper."

"You got it," she said.

"Supper for my wife too," he said.

"But no kids," Ma said.

"Just the oldest boy," he said.

"How old?" she said.

"Fourteen," he said.

"Then knock off a dollar," Ma said.

"He's small for his age," he said.

"Nine dollars," said Ma. "There'll be cigars too."

"Done and done," said the rabbi.

"Wear a yarmulka," said Ma.

Finally there was only one item left: target practice for Libbie. I'm talking about the bouquet brides always throw when they leave the wedding. To make sure it hit the right person here's what Ma did:

She stationed Libbie at one end of the living room and at the other end she set up the dressmaker's dummy with Celeste's pink taffeta formal on it. Then she gave Libbie a bouquet and made her practice till she was hitting the dummy ten times out of ten. Unless somebody else showed up in a pink taffeta formal, Celeste was a cinch.

Chapter Eleven

At last came Sunday, November the 8th, 1936, Libbie's wedding day. I put on a big smile in honor of the occasion but I'll be honest with you: inside I was dying, *really* dying, on account of this terrible tragedy that just happened about me and Bridget. I mean this was a *new* tragedy, on top of all the others I already told you.

What happened was two days before Libbie's wedding Bruce Albright limped up to me on campus and gave a smirk and said, "Hey, Morris, take a look at my sweater."

"Never mind the cute tricks," I said. "If you want to hit me, hit me."

"I don't want to hit you," he said. "Just look at my sweater is all."

I looked. "So?" I said.

"Notice something missing?" he said.

"What?" I said.

"My frat pin," he said. "Guess who's wearing it?"

"You're lying!" I hollered, but I knew he wasn't.

"No, Morris," he said. "Bridget is mine now, so what do you say we shake hands and show there's no hard feelings?"

"Shove it," I said. I'm not known for good sportsmanship. I walked away from Bruce and went and wrote a note to Bridget and put it in her P.O. box. Here's what I said:

> Dear Bridget,
> I love you and I always will. That's why I think you should know that Bruce Albright screws chickens and his father is a famous abortionist.
>
> Sincerely
> Morris Katz

So I got in a final zinger, but a fat lot of comfort that was. I was really in the crapper this time, no question. Here was Bridget wearing that putz's pin, and there was Crip still laying in a cast in Rochester and God knew when he'd get loose, and I couldn't find anyone else to write me a poem or any safe place to steal one. So what did that leave? Gloom and misery, that's what.

Still, this was no time to be kvetching around with a long face. It was Libbie's wedding day after all, even if she was getting stuck with a wrongo like Jonathan so, as I say, I put on a big smile and squared my shoulders and tried not to look how I felt. And actually—you'll excuse me but I got to say it—I did look pretty damn good. I'm not bragging; it was my cousin You-Know-Who's tux that did it. This was the first time in my life I'd ever worn a tux and I learned a big lesson: If you want people to think you got the world by the ass, put on a tux. Somehow it makes you seem tall and high-class and what they call *debonair*, even when you're five feet six with a hook nose and a broken heart.

Anyhow here it was Libbie's wedding day at last. The

ceremony was set for 5 P.M. so we got to the Lowry Hotel around three-thirty and Ma lined us up in the lobby and gave everybody their assignment. Libbie was to go to the room where brides get dressed and wait for Ma to come and help her. Ma was to go to the Grand Ballroom and make sure everything was ready for the wedding. I was to go along with Ma in case it was necessary to read something in English. ("I forgot my glasses," Ma said.) And Pa, since he had nothing else to do, was to look for the hotel's employment office and ask if maybe they were hiring some painters. "And don't get lost," Ma told Pa because he got such a tendency, especially when the building is higher than one story.

So Ma clapped her hands and we all went where she she said. I walked with Ma into the Grand Ballroom which looked to me in great shape. Everything was set up for the wedding—chairs, tables, bandstand, bar, and buffet. And also the chupah which is a silk canopy on four poles that Jews get married under. Over near the doorway the manager of the hotel, a bald head named Quistholm, was supervising some flunkeys who were putting on the finishing touches.

"Nu, Quistholm?" said Ma. "Still potchking around?"

"We are just finishing, madam," said Quistholm, looking at Ma like he wanted to bite her in the throat. He'd been doing business with her for the last three weeks so naturally he hated her. "Come along, men," he said to the flunkeys.

"Not so fast, Oscar of the Waldorf," said Ma, grabbing him by the carnation. "*This* is how you fix up a room?" Then she had him move a few hundred things around, especially if they were heavy. It took forty minutes before she ran out of ideas.

"Will this at long last be all?" said Quistholm. I don't know how he could talk with his mouth so tight together.

"Go," said Ma. "I'll rearrange the flowers myself."

So Quistholm walked out muttering old Norse curses and Ma rearranged the flowers. Next she walked over to the bandstand where Ralph Rifkin and his Rhythm Ramblers, all of them dressed in green jackets and gold pants except Rifkin who was dressed in a gold jacket and green pants, were unpacking their instruments.

"Nu, Rifkin?" said Ma.

Rifkin just gave a sigh. He wasn't any happier to see her than Quistholm. Neither were the Rhythm Ramblers.

"You didn't forget what I told you?" said Ma.

"No, Mrs. Katz," said Rifkin. "For the fast numbers we play 'Hava Nagilah.' For the slow numbers we play 'A Brivelleh de Mammeh.'"

"You got it," said Ma.

"Please, Mrs. Katz," he said, almost crying, "couldn't we throw in just a little Irving Berlin? He's Jewish."

"Who ever heard of him?" said Ma. "You'll play like I said."

"Yes, Mrs. Katz," he said. I never saw anybody look so unhappy in a gold jacket.

"And be sure you all got handkerchiefs," said Ma. "You sweat pretty good."

Next she went over to the chupah to see Rabbi Pflaum. For him she had only one question: "You remember your lines?"

"See here, my good woman," he said, getting red, but

Ma didn't stop to listen. "I'll go dress Libbie now," she said to me. "You find Pa. He's lost."

She was right. He'd made a wrong turn somewheres and ended up at a dinner-dance of the German-American Bund. Naturally he was too scared to ask anyone how to get out so he just crouched against the wall with a stein of beer in front of his face. I wasn't too anxious to go inside myself, but I managed to catch Pa's eyes from the doorway and he snuck out and followed me back to the Grand Ballroom. Just in time too because the first guests were arriving: my Uncle Benny and Aunt Esther and along with them, the crazy old grandmothers, Nutty Nettie and Little Gittel.

Now, I'm sure every family got a crazy old grandmother or two stashed away somewheres, but what made Nettie and Gittel a little different was nobody knew for sure whose grandmothers they were. We knew they belonged to *somebody* in our family, that much we agreed, but who? There was no use trying to ask the old ladies because they were both way over a hundred years old, some said a hundred and fifty, and they'd been bughouse for as long as anyone could remember. So the family argued back and forth and finally came to the conclusion that the best evidence pointed at Uncle Benny and Aunt Esther, so that's who Nettie and Gittel had been living with since 1920.

From the beginning Uncle Benny and Aunt Esther kept screaming it was all a horrible mistake, they weren't even related to the old ladies, but naturally everybody turned a deaf ear. Who wanted to get stuck with Nettie and Gittel? Believe me, they were more trouble than a pair of otters. They weren't like your average old nutsy person who just lays around the house and maybe drools a little. No, these two were *goers*. That's all they wanted —go, go, go, every minute. It didn't matter where: a wedding, a funeral, a trip to the butcher shop; any place you took them they'd sing and dance and holler and have a perfectly wonderful time.

The trouble came when you tried to take them home. I don't mean they'd cry or throw tantrums; that wasn't their style. What they'd do is grab a hold of something solid like a radiator or a doorjamb and you'd need at least four strong men to pry them loose.

And when you finally did get them home, all they could think of was escaping. Their favorite way was hitching trucks, which wasn't so bad if it was a local truck because generally the driver would find them when he finished his route and he'd bring them home by nightfall. But God knew how long it might take to get them back when they managed to grab onto a long hauler. In fact, that's what finally pushed Aunt Esther to the end of her rope, the day last August when the old ladies hopped a moving van to Winnipeg. "Okay, that does it," said Aunt Esther when the Mounties brought Nettie and Gittel home, and right there and then she crawled into her bed and announced she was going to lay there and die unless the family took the old ladies off her hands.

Well, Ma called a meeting right away because Aunt Esther was a real hardhead and when she said she was going to die, that's exactly what she was going to do, no question. So the family met and came to a decision: they

would put Nettie and Gittel into the Jewish Home for the
Aged and Infirm.

This, of course, had been suggested many times before
but it had never gotten off the ground because it would
cost $200 to stick Nettie and Gittel in the Home and no-
body wanted to kitty up their share of the money, especially since they all claimed not to be related. But
now with Aunt Esther's ultimatum, the family saw they
couldn't keep screwing around so they finally agreed to
chip in, share and share alike.

So they deposited $200 at the Home and Nettie and
Gittel got put on the official waiting list. As soon as a
couple beds opened up, they'd be admitted. Nobody
knew exactly when that would be, maybe a month, maybe
six months, because the waiting list was long and the
oldies at the Home weren't cashing in nearly as fast as
we hoped. Still, for the first time since 1920 Uncle Benny
and Aunt Esther finally knew that sooner or later they
were going to crawl out from under, and believe me, it
was one hell of a blessing.

So anyhow here they were, Nutty Nettie and Little
Gittel, in the Grand Ballroom of the Lowry Hotel, neither
of them higher than my waist, both dressed in kerchiefs
and black dresses that touched the floor, the same dresses
they always wore even when they were robbing birds'
nests, and they grabbed me each one by a lapel and
they looked up at me and grinned and giggled and
batted their eyes.

"Shaner, shaner, shaner boychik," said Nettie to me.
"You should live and be healthy. Here's for you a fountain
pen."

"Thank you, Grandma Nettie," I said, taking the pen. If she thought it was my bar mitzvah, so what?

"You got maybe a cookie?" said Gittel.

"There'll be lots of cookies later, Grandma Gittel," I said. "Ice cream too."

"God bless you, dolly," said Gittel. "Let's dance."

"After while, I promise," I said.

"Look what a pretty person," said Nettie, pointing at Ralph Rifkin. "Come, we'll give him a few kisses."

And off they rushed to the bandstand.

"Your fountain pen?" I said to Uncle Benny.

"Whose else?" he said, taking it back.

"Don't touch those drums, you old bats," hollered Aunt Esther and went running after Nettie and Gittel. So did Uncle Benny.

Now a lots of other guests started showing up but Ma came back from dressing Libbie and took over the job of greeting. Pa and I had other jobs. Me being best man, I had to escort Jonathan to the chupah and Pa, being father of the bride, had to escort Libbie.

So Pa and I left the Grand Ballroom and went to the dressing rooms where Libbie and Jonathan were. I looked in on Libbie for a minute to see if she had fainted again. She'd been doing it about once every half an hour since morning. Sure enough, there she was passed out cold so I waved her bouquet under her nose like Ma told me. Ma had sprinkled a good stiff dose of ammonia on the flowers.

Just then Celeste Zimmerman, the maid of honor, came walking in with the pink taffeta formal. "Hi, there," I said.

Her eyes popped wide open when she saw me. "Why, Morris," she hollered, "you look beautiful!"

"I know," I said. "It's the tux."

"It certainly makes a terrific improvement," she said.

"Yes, don't it?" I said.

"I can hardly wait to get my hands on you," she said. "How soon will this dumb wedding be over?"

"Not too late," I said.

"I hope not," she said. "You look beautiful."

"Thanks," I said.

"Where am I?" said Libbie, coming to.

"Hi, Lib," I said. "How do you feel?"

"Oh, Morris, I'm so happy!" she said and passed out again.

"Here, Pa, keep this under her nose," I said and gave him the bouquet. "Well, I'll see you folks later," I said and went to Jonathan's dressing room.

He was in a tux too and he looked even greater than I did. He sat in a chair tilted against the wall, pitching cards into a hat across the room. And not missing either. "Hi, kid," he said, giving me a smile. "How they hanging?"

"For a bridegroom you don't seem very nervous," I said. "Or maybe you've done this a few times already?"

"Oh, Morris, Morris," he said, shaking his head, "will you ever learn to trust me?"

"Maybe," I said. "We live a long time in my family. Take Nettie and Gittel."

"Here's the ring, you prick," he said, handing me a gold wedding band full of shiny chips that might even have been diamonds. "Don't lose it."

"Nice ring," I said. "Where'd you get it?"

"I cut off a lady's finger in a streetcar," he said.

"I believe you," I said.

"Nu, how's about a little pinochle while we wait?" he said, taking the cards out of the hat.

"If I can deal," I said.

"Oh, Morris, Morris," he said, shaking his head again, but he let me deal. He won anyhow.

At five o'clock we heard the orchestra start "Here Comes the Bride" which was our cue, so Jonathan and I went into the side door of the Grand Ballroom and got under the chupah with Rabbi Pflaum and faced the audience. There was an aisle leading from the chupah to the main entrance of the ballroom and on both sides of the aisle sat the wedding guests, at least a hundred and fifty people anyhow, of who I knew maybe 10 per cent. The rest were doctors, lawyers, accountants, and other strangers Ma had invited to give a little more class to the wedding.

So they sat with their heads turned backwards, looking up the aisle for the bride to appear, and Ralph Rifkin kept playing "Here Comes the Bride" and by and by the procession started. First, Celeste, the maid of honor, came marching down the aisle. There were a few laughs but mostly everyone was quiet. Then came Libbie, clutching Pa's arm. I don't know what was whiter, Libbie or her dress, but she kept sniffing her bouquet and she made it to the chupah. Behind Libbie, holding the train of her dress, was my eight-year-old cousin Evelyn, a terrible little shit who won the Jewish Shirley Temple contest last year and now she couldn't stop twinkling and tossing her curls.

Anyhow Libbie got to the chupah and switched from Pa's arm to Jonathan's which was a good thing because Pa was about to pass out himself. Then we all turned around and faced Rabbi Pflaum and the ceremony began.

I'd say the ceremony went very nicely except for a couple minor disturbances from the audience. One came from Nettie and Gittel naturally. The poor old things got a little mixed up about what was happening, but they could see it was a celebration of some kind so they picked the happiest song they could think of—"Jingle Bells"—and sang it all through the service. I mean loud. The other disturbance was Mrs. Zimmerman, Celeste's mother, who took a look at Celeste and me standing together under the chupah and busted out crying. And it wasn't the kind of crying people usually do at a wedding; it was more like a dog that just lost a beloved master. Mr. Zimmerman kept giving her an elbow in the ribs but that only made things worse because the elbow beating against her corset sounded like a tom-tom.

But otherwise it was a nice ceremony, a little fast maybe, but for nine bucks Rabbi Pflaum wasn't going to throw in any extras. So it was over one, two, three, and Libbie and Jonathan stamped on their wine glasses and kissed each other and everybody came crowding around the bride and groom to give mazeltov.

Pretty soon came a chord from the orchestra and Ralph Rifkin stepped to the microphone. "Good evening, ladies and gentlemen," he said. "Dancing is about to begin and of course we all know, don't we, what lucky couple are going to have the honor of dancing the first dance all by themselves?"

"Of course," said Ma, and as Rifkin gave the downbeat, she grabbed A. M. Zimmerman and pulled him out to the middle of the dance floor. And she kept him there too, no matter how hard he struggled, just the two of them dancing till the song was over.

I couldn't hear what Ma and Mr. Zimmerman were talking about while they danced because they were twirling by too fast—it was the *"Hava Nagilah"*—but I did manage to catch a couple of lines. "Nu, Zimmerman," Ma said, "you see what kind of classy people I got by my wedding?"

"I don't give a shit if you got FDR coming to sing 'I Love You Truly,'" said Mr. Zimmerman. "Celeste ain't gonna marry that cockaroach."

Which didn't sound like Ma was off to a flying start exactly. But I wasn't worried; Ma had cracked tougher nuts than old Zimmerman in her time. And besides, I was doing just fabulous with Celeste. That tux of mine really knocked her for a loop. She kept staring at me with pop eyes and breathing fast and yanking on my sleeve. "Let's get out of here, for cry-yi," she said. "I'm hornier than a billy goat."

"We got to wait till Libbie and Jonathan take off," I said.

"For where?" she said.

"The honeymoon," I said.

"Where they spending this honeymoon?" she said.

"Upstairs," I said. "Ma made the hotel throw in a double room with the deal."

"Where they gonna live afterwards?" said Celeste.

"With us," I said. "Naturally."

"How awful!" she said.

"Well, at least they got a hotel room tonight," I said.

"Hey, let's you and me get a hotel room tonight too," she said. "It must be even better than a car."

"That's what I hear," I said. "But who got three dollars?"

"Me," said Celeste.

"Okay," I said.

"Tell your sister to get the lead out," said Celeste.

"I'll try," I said, but I found out there was no way to hustle Libbie. Crying and kissing people were Libbie's two favorite things and she'd never had this many chances in her life.

After my mother and Mr. Zimmerman finished their solo, the dancing became general and the food and drinks were brought in, featuring my Aunt Bryna's specialty, a Star of David in blue and white chopped liver, and everyone started in having a good time, except of course for Celeste who kept looking at her watch and jerking my sleeve and Mr. Zimmerman who couldn't break loose from Ma's wristlock. And naturally, Mrs. Zimmerman, who hung on to a sconce and never stopped howling.

Celeste and I danced a little but not much, not together anyhow, because the minute we got out on the dance floor Nettie and Gittel came tearing over and cut in. "I'll take the boychik," Nettie said to Gittel, "and you take the fatty." So Nettie got me and Gittel waltzed away with Celeste. They must have kept us dancing for a full hour, including intermissions when the orchestra wasn't even there, before Uncle Benny and Aunt Esther came and rescued us. After that Celeste and I stayed off the dance floor and waited at the bar for the bride and groom to leave.

Celeste and I were pretty much alone at the bar because except for a few exceptions like Rummy Rosenberg who I've mentioned, your average Jew is no drinker. With such heartburn, how can he? But now and then somebody dropped by. Aunt Lena came over and tried to pin up Celeste's brassiere straps so they wouldn't keep falling out, but it didn't work. Uncle Shimen came by and asked Celeste if she'd ask her father if he could use an usher. My little cousin Evelyn came by and sang "The Good Ship Lollipop" till Celeste gave her a kick.

My cousin Albert sat with us for a while too but he didn't talk much. He was in a lousy mood. He'd had a date to bring to the wedding, a broad named Thelma Greenspan with ankles like a percheron who he met at school, but it turned out she didn't come with him after all. What happened was still another case of Albert's shitty luck. On his way over to pick up this Thelma, Albert had a few errands to do, like get a haircut, buy some rubbers, and steal some gas for his car. But he left himself plenty of time and he got to Thelma's house right on schedule. So she took him inside to meet her mother and father, and right there is where it ended.

Because who do you think her father was? The druggist who sold Albert the rubbers, that's who.

So Celeste and I sat at the bar waiting for Libbie and Jonathan to leave which took longer than we expected because Jonathan got busy analyzing handwriting for the guests, but finally it came time. Ralph Rifkin gave a drum roll (actually he was going to do a cymbal clash but Nettie and Gittel had stolen his cymbals) and he announced that the bride and groom were about to exit. So everybody grabbed a handful of rice and went rushing over to the staircase at the end of the room where Libbie and Jonathan were standing on the top.

Ma knocked down ten or twelve people and got Celeste positioned right smack in the front of the crowd so she'd be sure and catch Libbie's bouquet. Then Ma got a a good grip on Nettie and Gittel so they couldn't jump up and intercept; those two had been known to leap as high as eight feet straight in the air. Then Ma gave Libbie a nod, and Libbie closed one eye, took aim, and flang the bouquet straight at Celeste, a perfect bull's-eye.

"Nu, Zimmerman," said Ma, "you saw it yourself. It's fate."

"Fate, my ass," said Mr. Zimmerman.

"Pew, do these flowers stink," said Celeste.

Then everybody started yelling mazeltov and throwing rice and during the confusion Celeste and I snuck downstairs and booked ourselves a room. (I registered as Mr. and Mrs. Bruce Albright. Ha-ha.)

Celeste and I were both a little unsure of ourself when we got to the room. She of course was a total amateur when it came to indoor humping, and I got to admit I wasn't too experienced either. I was, as you know, a highly skilled car humper but I hadn't done much of it in rooms except for those few times at Cockeye Jennie's, but they were only ten-minute tricks, not nearly enough time to learn the fine points. So you could say the both of us were kind of feeling our way.

"Well, I guess the first thing is we take off all our clothes," said Celeste.

"No," I said, "I think the first thing is we tip the bell-boy."

"That's the way I'd do it, folks," said the bellboy.

So Celeste gave him a dime and he left.

"Okay," she said, "now we take off all our clothes, right?"

"Shouldn't we talk a little bit first?" I said.

"Why can't we talk while we're taking off all our clothes?" she said.

"We could do that, I guess," I said.

So we started in undressing. "I love you," I said.

"Well, I hope you do, Morris," she said, "but even if you don't, I'm sure looking forward to this."

"Me too," I said. "And pretty soon, mark my words, we'll be having a real wedding night of our own."

"Not if Daddy can help it," she said.

"Don't worry, you'll soften him up," I said.

"I wouldn't count on it," she said.

"I would," I said which was the God's truth. I was counting heavily on it. In fact, I'd already decided that if I lost both Bridget and the Zimmerman money, I was going to borrow Albert's car and monoxide myself.

"See if you can unloosen this zipper," said Celeste. "If you can't, just rip the dress up the side."

"I got it," I said.

"Thanks," she said. "You want some help with that collar button?"

"Thanks," I said and in a couple minutes we finished undressing and looked each other over.

"To be honest I liked you better in the tux," she said.

"Look who's talking," I said.

"Yes, I know," she said. "I'm sorry I haven't got a prettier body for you, Morris."

"Not your fault," I said. "A person got to play the hand they're dealt."

"That's how I feel," she said. "And besides it's not such a bad body."

"Oh?" I said.

"I'm talking medically," she said. "It never gets sick and it never gets tired and it loves food and sex. Would I be better off if I was beautiful and puny?"

"That's a very mature attitude," I said.

"Well, let's get cracking," she said.

"Okay," I said.

"Don't spend too much time on pre-coital play," she said. "I'm already ready."

"Okay," I said, and we gave it a go.

This was one of the nights when I had no trouble getting it up, thank God, so I didn't have to close my eyes and imagine movie stars. I was able to pay full attention to what was going on, and I picked up a lot of interesting information I never knew about room humping. First of all, when it comes to comfort and warmness, a room got a car beat all hollow. I mean it's just no contest. But on the other hand there's a big disadvantage too: you can't drive anywheres after you finish and there's nothing to do when a hump is over except start another one so you end up tearing off a lot more pieces than you had in mind actually.

But Celeste enjoyed it which I was glad for because after all, she had a lot of money tied up in that room. To her it was worth every penny. She just kept yelling, "Ride 'em, cowboy!" and loving each draggy hour. It was four o'clock in the morning before I finally persuaded her we should go home.

"Well, Morris," she said as we got dressed, "I want you to know this was the swellest evening of my life. So far, that is."

"Likewise," I said.

"I'm gonna ask Daddy for three dollars so we can get a room again," she said.

"I wouldn't tell him what the money's for," I said.

"You seen a bust pad anywheres?" she said.

"Here in the bedclothes," I said. "Also your glasses."

"Thanks," she said. "Well, let's go."

"Your dress is on backwards," I said.

"Oh, phooey," she said and took it off. "Listen," she said, "as long as it's off, how about one more you-know?"

"Well, I guess one more won't hurt," I said.

So I squeezed out another one and then she took me home and walked me to the door. "Rest up good," she said. "Nighty-night."

"Nighty-night," I said and she went back to her car and drove off to Minneapolis whistling.

I stood on the porch thinking for a couple minutes after Celeste was gone. And I got to say I was thinking very clearly in spite of how late it was and all I'd been through. Or maybe that helps. Maybe when the old pecker runs down, the old brain finally gets a chance.

Anyhow, these were the thoughts I thought: First about Celeste: Obviously she was nobody whose picture you pasted in your locker, but still and all, there were lots of worse broads around, lots of poorer ones for sure. And I *had* Celeste now; that was the point. All I had to do is play it careful and I'd soon be up to my poopik in Zimmerman money.

So why keep chasing Bridget? Wasn't it time already to wipe the yum-yum out of my eyes and see things the way they really were? Celeste I had, Bridget I never would, and only a half-wit would keep on trying.

So right there on the front porch at four-thirty in the morning, thinking clearly for a change, I finally made up my mind: no more Bridget. It hurt. Believe me, it hurt. It hurt so bad I almost couldn't do it. But I did. I made my decision and then I gave a sigh and blew my nose and went into the house wondering what it was going to be like, life without happiness.

Chapter Twelve

Well, life goes on, happiness or not.

Libbie and Jonathan moved in with us the day after the wedding as you know, and although I was more dead than alive on account of giving up Bridget, I still couldn't help looking forward to next Sunday morning. It was on Sunday mornings, you'll remember, when that big bull-shitter Jonathan told us he went around to all those beer joints and made a fortune blowing out beer coils with his little red hose. So naturally I could hardly wait to see what would happen. Ma too.

Sure enough, at 9 A.M. on Sunday Jonathan stuck that little red hose in his pocket, kissed Libbie, and said, "So long, folks. I'll be back in a flash with the cash."

"Yeh, yeh," said Ma and me, both of us wondering what excuse he'd have when he came home. Well, imagine our surprise when he walked in a few hours later, whipped off his hat, made a bow, and said to Ma, "Here you are, Madame Queen." Then he turned the hat over on Ma's lap and out fell a mess of singles and change, twenty-three dollars it came to!

"And here's for you, my blushing bride," said Jonathan to Libbie and handed her a six-ounce bottle of Djer Kiss perfume. So she busted out crying naturally.

Then he gave Pa and me each a half-pound Mr. Good-bar, and he started the entertainment. What a guy, that Jonathan! Crooked as an S-hook, no question, but by God wherever he was, was a party! You should have seen him this time. He sang, he danced, he juggled, he opened a bottle of pop with his armpit, and he gave some terrific imitations. The best one, I think, was Helen Keller carving a duck. Everybody got hysterical, even Ma who hated Jonathan, and me who was more dead than alive on account of giving up Bridget.

Later Jonathan and I got a chance to talk private for a couple minutes. Ma and Libbie were in the kitchen cooking supper and Pa was in the bedroom changing pants; he'd wet himself a little bit from laughing.

"Well, Jonathan," I said to him, "I suppose I ought to keep my mouth shut and just enjoy your wonderful talent, but I'm dying from curiosity. So I'm gonna ask you once more. What the hell does a guy like you expect to get from a crappy outfit like us?"

"Morris," he said, "even if I told you, you wouldn't understand."

"Why not?" I said.

"Because you're still too young and full of fancy ideas," he said. "Now don't get me wrong. I admire it; I really do. I was the same way myself once—brave and hopeful, chasing rainbows, pissing against wind. You think you're the only one who ever dreamed about marrying a rich broad?"

"But I'm gonna," I said. "There's the difference."

"I hope so," he said. "I'm hoping and praying and holding my left nut for you, kid."

"But?" I said.

"But let's be a little realistic here," he said. "When shleppers tangle with millionaires, don't count your chickens. I'll tell you something from long experience: guys like you and me only got one way to win: steal small."

"Oh, yeah?" I said. "Well, it just so happens that Celeste is in the bag practically."

"Marvelous," he said. "Wonderful. Nobody's rooting harder than me, you know that. But meanwhile it's gonna hurt if you start looking around in a lower bracket also? Listen, for a broad who's worth three, four thousand net, you'd be a very sensible buy."

"Thanks a peck," I said.

"I mean it," he said. "Now you take Libbie's friend, Ruthie Baumgarten, for example. Don't make faces, Morris. It's so terrible, a registered nurse?"

"She is also a registered harelip," I said.

"So?" he said.

"So good-by," I said because what's the use arguing with a closed mind? Let Jonathan steal small if he wanted to; I knew I was going to end up with Celeste Zimmerman. In fact, I *really* knew it a little while later when she came over to get me in the Olds. Because she said an unbelievable thing.

"Morris," she said, "Daddy told me I should bring you to his office."

"You sure he meant *me?*" I said.

"He said, 'Bring the cockaroach,'" said Celeste.

"What do you suppose he wants?" I said.

"He wouldn't tell," she said. "My guess is he's gonna offer you some money to stop seeing me."

"Well, I sure hope he don't try anything like that," I said and I wasn't kidding. I was afraid if he went as high as twelve dollars I'd grab it.

So we drove over to the Majestic Theatre in Minneapolis where Zimmerman had his office. The Majestic was the biggest and busiest of the Zimmerman theaters but I'll tell you something: there were no lines standing there tonight. A stinkeroo called *Dodsworth* was playing with Walter Huston and Ruth Chatterton and if those two are movie stars, I say there's a chance for my Aunt Bryna and Uncle Herschel too.

"Tickets, please," said the doorman.

"Hi, Sven," I said because it was the former butler. "Glad to see you working again."

"Thank you, young master," he said. "It's not the same of course, but one does what one must. Good evening, Miss Celeste."

"In here," said Mr. Zimmerman, leaning out of his office, so we went in.

Mr. Zimmerman had a different expression on his face tonight. Usually when he saw me he got the same look—disgust with rage is the way to describe it, I think—but tonight he looked mostly confused. Disgusted and raged too, but mostly confused.

"I got something to say," he said. "So shut up and listen."

"Before you begin," I said, "I want you to know I love Celeste and all the money in the world would never make me leave her."

"You wanna listen or you wanna bullshit?" he said.

"Listen," I said.

"Okay," he said. "Morris, I'm gonna level with you."

"Ho-ho-ho," said Celeste.

"I mean it," said Mr. Zimmerman. "Something terrible happened yesterday."

"What?" I said.

"I went by my doctor for a checkup," he said. "He found a lump."

"Where," I said.

"In my wallet, putz," he said. "Will you shut up and listen?"

"Yes," I said. "I'm sorry about the lump."

"Don't be sorry, it was only suet," he said. "All the same it makes a man think. Who knows when they're gonna get called?"

"Especially so fat," I said.

"Naturally I'm still hoping Celeste will stop this bullshit and throw you out," he said.

"Oh, I'm sure I will eventually," said Celeste. "But what's the big hurry?"

"See, Morris, what I'm up against?" said Mr. Zimmerman. "But I'm fighting you, don't worry, I'm fighting you till I drop. In fact, I'm going next week by my lawyer and making a codicil on my will. You know what's a codicil?"

"What?" I said.

"A codicil is Celeste don't get a goddam penny if she marries you," he said.

"Mr. Zimmerman," I said, "even a monster wouldn't do such a thing to an only child."

"Aha, now you put your finger on it," said Mr. Zimmerman. "I'm gonna make the codicil, sure. But maybe you're right. Maybe in the end I'll weaken and change it back."

"So why make it in the first place?" I said. "Running up all those lawyer bills and everything?"

"Because I ain't gonna weaken," said Mr. Zimmerman. "You know anybody around town who calls me soft-hearted?"

"Nobody," I said.

"And don't you forget it," he said. "Still and all, a man got to be prepared for the worst. So in case, God forbid, you *do* marry Celeste and in case I *don't* chase the both of you out in the street—I *will*, don't worry, but I'm talking *in case*—then I better start getting you ready."

"Ready for what?" I said.

"To be a son-in-law," he said. "You begin working for me tonight."

"Well, well," I said, giving myself a mazeltov, because finally the old sonofabitch had said the magic word—*son-in-law*. Let him threaten all he wanted with his codicils; I had my foot in the door now and we both knew it.

"Okay, enough bullshit," he said. "Go on over to my Fine Arts Theatre right away. There's a kid named Rex taking tickets, about your size. Tell him he's fired and put on his uniform."

"You wanna talk about salary?" I said.

"You'll take what I give you," he said.

"That seems fair," I said and Celeste and I drove over to the Fine Arts Theatre where after a little crying this kid Rex finally gave up his uniform. It fitted me nice.

Chapter Thirteen

Naturally Albert was pleased when I told him the news about my job with Zimmerman. "I am proud and thrilled, Morris," he said. "Now let me tell you something as your closest friend and relation. If you blow it again this time, I will murdalize you."

"Don't worry," I said.

"I'll worry," he said. "I'll worry because I know you're still honing for this Bridget cooz, aren't you?"

"A little maybe," I said.

"How did I get such a schmuck for a cousin?" he said.

"Albert," I said, "I've given up on Bridget, honest to God I have. But that don't mean I can just kick her out of my mind."

"You got to," he said.

"Yeah?" I said. "You wouldn't talk so cocky if you'd ever been in love yourself."

"Well," said Albert, "I guess I better tell you something I was never gonna."

"What?" I said.

"I been," he said.

"In *love?*" I said, giving him a look.

"What's the matter, you think you invented it?" he said.

"Why didn't you ever tell me before?" I said.

"If you knew who the broad was, you wouldn't have to ask," he said.

"So who?" I said.

"This is real embarrassing," he said.

"Come on, Albert," I said.

"I don't think I can tell you," he said.

"Albert, you can't do this to a person," I said. "Now come on."

"All right," he said. "You remember in John Marshall Junior High we had a penmanship teacher Miss Stapleton?"

"So?" I said.

"Her," he said.

"Are you nuts?" I hollered. "She was a hundred years old."

"She was twenty-eight," he said.

"So you were fourteen," I said.

"Fifteen," he said. "But so what? I loved her, that's all."

"Oh, come on," I said. "That's not love. That's what they call puppy love."

"Oh, yeah?" he said. "Well, Miss Stapleton had it too."

"She loved *you?*" I said.

"That's what she told me," he said.

"When?" I said.

"Every time I fucked her," he said.

"Oh, my God!" I said, getting white. "Where'd you do that?"

"In her flat," said Albert. "Where did you think—the cafeteria?"

"How long did this go on?" I said.

"The whole ninth grade," he said.

"Albert, this is craziness," I said. "A *penmanship teacher?*"

"You don't know the worst," he said. "We were gonna get married as soon as I turned sixteen."

"Oh, my God!" I hollered. "What happened?"

"Well, one day we were up at her flat screwing," he said, "and there was a knock on the door. 'Who is it?' hollers Miss Stapleton. 'Wanna buy a *Liberty Magazine?*' comes a voice, a woman's voice. 'Just a minute, I'll be right there,' hollers Miss Stapleton. But I grab her. 'Miss Stapleton,' I say, 'please don't go.' Because I knew right away who was out there."

"Your mother?" I said.

"Who else?" said Albert.

"So why didn't you tell Miss Stapleton?" I said.

"Would you like to tell somebody *your* mother is peddling magazines?" said Albert.

"I see what you mean," I said. "So what did you do?"

"I says to her, 'Miss Stapleton, please don't go. What do you need with a *Liberty?*' So she says, 'I'm keeping up with a serial.' And before I can stop her, she puts on a kimono and finds a nickel and goes to the door."

"So your mother sees you?" I said.

"No, I was in the bedroom," he said.

"Well, that was lucky," I said.

"But my goddam Golden Gloves jacket was in the front hall," he said.

"Oh-oh," I said.

"Ma had Miss Stapleton on the next train out of St. Paul," he said. "In the kimono."

"And a damn good thing, I say," I said.

"I say it too," said Albert. "*Now* I say it. Just like you'll say it some day about this Bridget cooz."

"You really think so, Albert?" I said.

"You'll forget her, Morris, I guarantee you," he said.

"Don't you ever think about Miss Stapleton any more?" I said.

"Sometimes when I'm doing Palmer Method," he said. "But it passes."

Well, if somebody had shagged Bridget out of town like Albert's mother shagged Miss Stapleton, maybe I would have got over her in time. I doubt it, but maybe. The trouble was nobody shagged Bridget. So one night a couple weeks later I was taking tickets at the Fine Arts and who should walk into the lobby but her! And not just her; her with her arm in that schmuck's elbow, Bruce Albright!

Well, talk about your frozen moment! Bridget gave a gasp. I gave a gasp. She stared. I stared. She turned pale. I turned pale. She turned red. I turned red.

Finally that schmuck Bruce spoke up: "You gonna take these tickets or what?" he said.

"Hello, Bridget," I said. "How you been?"

"Fine, thank you," she said. "And you?"

"Tip-top," I said. "So what's new?"

"Nothing much," she said.

"Hey, Shorty, I'm talking to you," Bruce said.

"You changed your hair a little," I said. To Bridget, not Bruce.

"Yes, a little," she said.

"It looks nice," I said.

"Thank you," she said.

"Of course the old way looked nice too," I said.

"You're asking for it," Bruce said.

"Well, it was good seeing you, Morris," Bridget said.

"Me too," I said. "Oh, by the way, my new poem is coming along just terrific."

(You see? There I was again, pissing up the same old rope. What poem? There was no poem; there never would be. So what happened to all those sensible decisions I made? Gone, that's what happened. Gone the second I saw her face, that wonderful face, and I only knew one thing: screw sensible; I loved this girl and I couldn't let her go, not yet, not without one more try at least.)

"Yes sir, the poem is coming along lickety-split," I said. "But you know what would help? If we could have a couple conferences."

"I'm not going to stand here and listen to this crap," said Bruce, getting red.

"So go someplace else," I said. "Who needs you?"

"That does it," he said and pulled back his arm but luckily it was the arm Bridget was hanging on. "Please, Bruce," she said, "let's find another movie."

"What for?" he said. "This is the one I want to see."

I couldn't blame him for that. It was *Pigskin Parade* with Stuart Erwin and Patsy Kelly, a laff riot.

"Please, Bruce," she said again.

He growled a little but finally he left with Bridget, thank God, and I stood there blinking my eyes. For a long time I blinked. Was I really doing what it looked like—picking fights with goyim six feet four inches, starting another hopeless chase after Bridget again? Yes, I really was.

And what if I did get Bridget back? Could I keep her? Of course not. Could I dump Celeste? Of course not? So what chance did I have? Only one: that Titania, queen of the fairies, would come in the middle of the night and stick a magic propellor in my ass so I could fly away with Bridget to an enchanted land beyond the sea.

In other words, don't hock me with sensible questions. All I can tell you is what I did, not why, and what I did was head for Rochester first thing next morning.

Chapter Fourteen

Naturally I was hoping Crip was recovered enough to write me a poem. He wasn't. All the same, he *had* made a terrific improvement. The great big mummy case was off of him completely now. The only casts he was wearing were two little ones. Of course with my luck they were both on his hands.

Still it was great to see him looking so much better and I told him so.

"Thanks, Morris," said Crip. "You should have seen me a couple days ago. I had no casts on at all."

"No kidding," I said.

"Yes," he said. "The doctor took off that big body cast and he examined me carefully, inch by inch, and he looked real pleased. So I said to him, 'Well, doc, what do you think?' So he said, 'Well, Walter, it's still too early to tell of course but at this point it looks good. So cross your fingers.' So I did, and you see what happened."

He held up the two casts.

I just gave a sigh; what else could I say?

"I guess you still need a poem, huh?" he said.

"Worse than ever," I said.

"Have you tried stealing one someplace?" he said.

"Every place," I said. "But I'm always afraid she'll recognize it. You wouldn't happen to know of some great poet nobody ever heard of, would you?"

"I'm afraid not, Morris," he said. "With great poets it's bound to get around."

"Yes, I can see that," I said.

"I know some *bad* poets nobody ever heard of," he said.

"That wouldn't help, I don't think," I said.

"I'm sorry, Morris," he said. "I wish I could do something for you."

"Listen," I said, "don't you worry about my little problems. Just take care of yourself and continue with your road to recovery."

"Thank you," he said.

"Well, I better get going," I said. "Anything I can tell your mother?"

"Yes, tell her thanks for the mangoes," he said.

"Sure thing," I said and waved and left.

Well, this time I was ready to quit, I really was. Wouldn't you be? And I would have quit, no question, except a couple days later, in my own kitchen of all places, right out of nowheres, all of a sudden the answer fell smack into my lap.

It happened on a Sunday morning a little past nine o'clock. Jonathan had just left the house with his mysterious magic red hose. He'd been going out now every Sunday morning since he married Libbie and always without fail he come home with at least twenty bucks so we knew it couldn't be poor boxes he was heisting. What it was we still didn't know, but by now nobody asked.

What the hell, a double sawbuck every Sunday and a floor show into the bargain, who could complain?

Anyhow, Jonathan was off on his evilness, and the rest of us were just lazing around the kitchen while Pa read the *Jewish Forward* out loud. Itzik Fishel's poem this week was real rip-snorter, full of tragedy and capitalist oppression and hollering. *Esther Resnick, American* it was called and I tell you, it just wrung out a person from emotion. So I sat and listened to Pa reading and —whammo!—all of a sudden there it was—my answer! There is was plain as day—the great poet nobody ever heard of. Itzik Fishel, who else? Why didn't I think of it a long time ago?

Well, naturally I was in a big rush to start in translating *Esther Resnick, American* from Yiddish into English, but Sunday was a busy day for me on account of continuous performances from 2 P.M. at the Fine Arts Theatre. So I didn't tackle the poem till the next day.

I'll tell you in a minute how it went, but first I'd like to say one thing: Thanks to Itzik Fishel, this poem *Esther Resnick, American* was absolutely loaded with power. I want to emphasize this point. That's one thing I did not have to do: put in power. That was there already, the power, and I'm glad to give the credit to where it belongs: Itzik Fishel.

But still and all, it was me who did the heavy part. I don't mean translating the poem from Yiddish; that was easy. But translating is one thing, and poetry is another. I'll show you what I mean. Here, exactly, is how the first stanza of the poem looked after I put it in English:

Woe is me, last night Esther Resnick killed herself!
Oh, woe, such a young person, sixteen years old that's all,
a baby yet,
With her own scissors she stabbed herself, you hear me?
Poor all her life and dead already, a curse on such a world!

Well, as you can see, it's got power to spare, no question. But go find a rhyme. Also where is what they call the *meter*?

So that's what I had to do, make rhymes and meter, and if you think that's simple, try it some time. All I can say is, if you're looking for light work stay out of the poetry business. Anyhow, take a look at the same first stanza after I fixed it up:

> *Last night a girl aged sixteen years,*
> *Named Esther Resnick, not J. P. Morgan,*
> *Took out her pair of pinking shears,*
> *And plunged them through a vital organ.*

All the difference in the world, right?

But as I say, I worked my ass off. That first stanza alone took me a whole half a day and the rest weren't any quicker. But finally after a hard couple weeks it was done and you'll excuse me if I say it, but I got to: it was a beaut. I knew it couldn't possibly fail with Bridget; I was absolutely positive. Now let me tell you why I didn't give it to her.

I got home from school the day I finished the poem—I hadn't given it to Bridget yet; I was going to make a nice clean copy and hand it to her tomorrow—and as Albert drove me up to my house we heard such hysterical screams coming from inside that we figured somebody was at least dead, so naturally we rushed in, the both of us.

I still can't describe exactly what we saw there, but I'll try to give you a general impression. In the middle of the living room was Jonathan with my four aunts standing around him all screaming like maniacs. "Scandal!" they were screaming. "Disgrace! Shame! Gevald!" Things like that they were screaming.

"Take it easy, girls, take it easy," Jonathan kept saying but they wouldn't. They just screamed and shook their fingers in his face and jumped up and down and got redder and redder till they looked like tomatoes.

Then they started belting him with their little pointy fists and that's when Libbie leapt in. "Anybody who touches my husband got to kill me first!" she hollered and flang her body across Jonathan's like Molly Pitcher or Barbara Fritcher or whatever the fuck her name was in the history book.

On the other side of the room my uncles were huddled together trying to look invisible like they always did when there was hollering. My father was with the uncles of course, also trying to look invisible, and he came the closest to making it.

Ma was pacing the whole length of the room, back and forth, forth and back, pacing fast, almost running, every once in a while giving Jonathan a glare, but not saying a word; she was too mad to talk.

And standing near the doorway, twirling his night stick, grinning, enjoying the whole show, was Officer Mulcahey, the cop from the Selby Avenue beat.

"What happened for God sakes?" I hollered.

It took a good ten minutes to get the answer because all the aunts were screaming so loud you couldn't hear any of them. But bit by bit I pieced it together. What happened was the truth had finally come out about where Jonathan was getting his money.

I'm ashamed I didn't figure it out from the very beginning, that's how obvious it was. I mean if a man is a crook and also a handwriting expert, isn't it obvious what kind of crookery he'd be doing? *Forgery*, of course.

Well, I'll tell you in one word how I felt when I learned the truth about Jonathan: *disappointed*. I don't mean I look down my nose at forgery. I certainly do not. It's a highly skilled business and there's big opportunities for people with shrewdness and boldness.

But Jonathan wasn't that kind of a forger. First of all, do you know whose signatures he was forging? My *uncles'*, for Christ sakes! Now, how's that for big-time thievery?

And second, the checks were so little, it was embarrassing. Jonathan would look for a corner grocery store in a faraway neighborhood where nobody knew him, and he'd walk in and start his usual line of wisecracks with the storekeeper and when he had him laughing real good, he'd con him into cashing a check—never more than a couple bucks naturally because how much can you get from a corner storekeeper even when he's laughing? So the grand total of Jonathan's whole crime came to a little over two hundred dollars, and I bet he walked a thousand blocks to get it.

Well, I really expected something classier from Jonathan. Here was a guy who'd been so many places, done so many things, knew so many stunts, a guy with *glamor* —I'm not ashamed to say it—so what does he wind up pulling? Forging my uncles on two dollar checks! I mean that's real chickenshit, even when your motto is "Steal small."

Plus on top of it, he goes and gets caught. And *easy* too. How much trouble could the cops have had with a description like this: thirty-five years old, six feet tall, a black moustache, a gold tooth, and a little red hose sticking out of his pocket?

So I told him how I felt. "Jonathan," I said, "I am disappointed."

"What did you expect?" he said. "The Lindbergh baby?"

"You shut up, goniff," said Ma to Jonathan, her first words; till now she'd just been pacing and glaring. Now she talked. "You shut up," she said, "and everybody else shut up too and sit down and listen. Officer Mulcahey, good-by. You we don't need here."

"Indeed, Mrs. Katz?" said Officer Mulcahey. "Then who'll be escorting Mr. Kaplan to jail?"

"Bite your tongue!" said Ma. "Kaplan ain't going to jail."

"Who then is going?" said Aunt Bryna. "Our husband?"

"*Nobody* is going," said Ma. "We're gonna pay back every penny."

"*Who* is?" said Aunt Ida.

"All of us," said Ma. "This is family business and the family got to stick together."

"Mother Katz is right," said Jonathan to the aunts. "So come on, girls, let's dig into them mattresses."

"You shut up," said Ma to Jonathan. "But he's right," she said to the aunts. "You got to borrow me two hundred dollars."

"Never!" hollered Aunt Lena. "Scheiss on Kaplan. Let him go to jail."

"Listen," hollered Ma, "you think *I* wouldn't like him in jail, that pascudnyak? I'd *love* him in jail. In the electric chair better yet. But Mr. Respectable Big Shot High Tone Zimmerman, that's all he needs to hear—a jailbird in the family—and it's good-by, Morris."

So the aunts stopped hollering and gave a sad nod because they knew it was true what Ma said.

"Okay, you see how it is, girls," said Jonathan to the aunts. "So how's about some volunteers? Just fifty bucks apiece and we got the whole two hundred."

"You shut up," said Ma to Jonathan. "But he's right," she said to the aunts. "Please, my sisters, my flesh and blood, borrow me the money. Libbie and Morris are both working. They'll pay you back, I promise, I don't care if it takes five years."

"So let Libbie and Morris pay back the storekeepers who got stuck with the checks," said Aunt Esther. "What do you need with us?"

"Ah, but there's the paradox, ladies, don't you see?" said Officer Mulcahey to the aunts.

"The what?" said the aunts.

"I mean," said Officer Mulcahey, "that if Mr. Kaplan here had been able to write more substantial checks—for fifty or a hundred dollars, let's say—his victims might be willing to wait a few years for their money instead of prosecuting. But for two dollars I'm afraid they feel very much as this lady here does." He turned to Aunt Lena. "What was it you said, madam?"

"I said, 'Scheiss on Kaplan. Let him go to jail,'" said Aunt Lena.

"There you are," said Officer Mulcahey. "Unless you can pay these storekeepers in full and immediately, I think you'll not be seeing Mr. Kaplan for a while."

"You hear that, girls?" said Jonathan. "We're not playing peesha-paysha here, so let's come up with the money, shall we?"

But the aunts just kept standing and looking sad.

"Pearl," said Aunt Ida to my mother, "you want my arm? Take. My leg? Take. Take anything. But money? We ain't got, that's all."

"Maybe somebody else would borrow you," said Aunt Bryna to Ma. "Don't you know nobody with a steady job?"

"Who?" said Ma, giving a shrug. Then all of a sudden her eyes popped wide open. "Hey, wait a minute!" she hollered.

"Oh, no!" hollered Officer Mulcahey because that's who Ma was looking at with the wide eyes. "I've seven growing children and a blind mother in Donegal."

So everybody went back to looking sad.

"Listen," said Jonathan, "this is serious. Ain't anybody here got anything they can sell, for Christ sakes?"

Nobody answered. For a second I thought Aunt Lena was going to say something but she didn't.

Officer Mulcahey cleared his throat. "I'm sorry about this, Mr. Kaplan," he said, "but I've my duty to do. You'll come quietly, I trust."

He took Jonathan by the arm. Libbie didn't make any problems because she fainted instantly. So Jonathan started walking across the room with Officer Mulcahey but he stopped just before they got to the door. "Officer," said Jonathan, "could I say one last word?"

"But of course," said Officer Mulcahey. "We're all humane and civilized people here, I hope."

"That's very kind," said Jonathan, and turned to Ma. "Mother Katz," he said, "I'd like to thank you for all your efforts and I want you to know I don't hold no grudges."

"Grudges!" hollered Ma. "*You* are talking grudges? After all you done?"

"All right, what did I do?" Jonathan hollered right back. "I'll tell you what: First of all I brought Libbie the greatest happiness she has ever known. Ask her when she comes to. Second, whatever money I scraped up, I shared fair and square. Didn't I hand you a hatful every Sunday? And third, haven't I kept everybody in stitches since I moved in? Has this family ever had so many laughs in your whole farkakte life?"

"He got a point there, Ma," I said.

"You shut up," Ma said.

"Thanks, Morris," Jonathan said. "You're a good kid and I wish I could be here to guide you in the difficult days ahead. Tell Libbie I'll write as often as they let me. For the rest of you—well, I guess the less said the better."

"Don't be too hard on them, Mr. Kaplan," said Officer Mulcahey. "I'm sure they *want* to help."

"Hah!" said Jonathan, giving this bitter laugh. "I'm ready, Officer."

But all of a sudden Aunt Lena jumped in front of them. "Wait!" she hollered.

So they waited.

Aunt Lena opened her mouth to talk just like she did before, but again she couldn't do it. Once more she tried, twice more, three times, and still she couldn't.

"Lena, what is it?" said Ma.

Finally she got the words out. "All right, Pearl," she said. "I'll borrow you the money."

"Fifty dollars?" said Ma.

"The whole two hundred," said Aunt Lena.

Everybody gave a gasp naturally.

"God bless you, you should live a hundred and twenty years with your husband and children together," said Ma. "Where you gonna get so much money?"

"For you I will sell my fur coat," said Aunt Lena.

"Oh, no!" shrieked Albert and I felt my knees buckling. In case you forgot, this was the fur coat Albert stole to pay his tuition.

"What kind of a *no?*" said Aunt Lena to Albert. "It's my sister, my flesh and blood."

"You can't!" shrieked Albert.

"Who says?" said Aunt Lena.

Albert looked this way and that way, like maybe there was help coming from somewheres but there wasn't. "Well, I guess this is it, Morris," said Albert to me.

"I guess so," I said.

So he told his mother.

You never heard such a silence.

"Would you like me to book the lad, madam?" said Officer Mulcahey to Aunt Lena. "I'm on my way to the station anyhow."

"*A hundred dollars?*" said Aunt Lena to Albert. "That's all you got for a Hudson seal in spotless condition? Come on home, I wanna talk to you."

"Don't go," said Ma. "Please, don't nobody go. You too, Kaplan. Everybody stay, I'm begging you. Sit down and help me think where to raise two hundred dollars."

"I know where," said Pa, which nobody expected, you can bet.

"*You?*" said Ma.

"The Jewish Home for the Aged and Infirm," said Pa. "Remember we deposited two hundred dollars to put Nettie and Gittel on the waiting list?"

"Oh, no!" screamed Aunt Esther. "Oh, no! No, God damn it, no! That money is to stick those old bats in the Home and that's where they're going the minute there's an opening. They are not gonna keep living with me. No, sir! No, no, no, no, no, no!"

"That's not what I'm saying," said Pa.

"Wait a minute, wait a minute," said Ma to Pa. "If you're saying what I think you're saying, don't say it."

"You got maybe a better idea?" said Pa.

Ma thought for a while. "No," she said at last and gave a sigh that shook the whole room. "Okay," she said, "so that's what I'll do."

"Wait a minute," hollered Aunt Esther.

"Never mind wait a minute," said Ma. "I'm taking back the two hundred dollars from the Home and Nettie and Gittel will come and live with me."

"Ma, don't do it!" I hollered.

"You shut up," said Ma. "You shut up and go eat your supper and then go to your job. And don't be late. And don't be sassy with Mr. Zimmerman. Also with Mrs. Zimmerman. And with Celeste you'll behave like Ronald Colman with Tyrone Powers together. Because just remember one thing, boychik: if God forbid you don't marry some money, I am stuck with Nettie and Gittel for the rest of their life. You know how long that could be?"

I didn't answer, just gave a shiver, because everybody knew Nettie and Gittel were good for another fifty years minimum. Why not? They had the electrocardiogram of a twelve-year-old kid and the digestion of a dog.

So right there and then I knew it was all over with Bridget, this time for sure. What kind of a rat would I be if I went after Bridget and lost Celeste and sentenced my own mother to fifty years with Nettie and Gittel? No, I just couldn't do it. So later that night I took my translation of Itzik Fishel's poem *Esther Resnick, American* and hid it away in the bottom of a drawer—a classic lost to the world just like Bridget was lost to me.

Chapter Fifteen

Nettie and Gittel moved in with us the next morning, and naturally the first thing they did was escape. And they kept right on. How they got out, don't ask me. The doors and windows were locked at all times. Pa's theory was they slipped through the mail slot and he might just be right.

Anyhow, for the first week there wasn't a single day when Officer Mulcahey didn't have to go looking for the old ladies. Most of the time, luckily, they didn't take very long to find because either they'd be in the spraying room at Formanek Brothers Auto Repainting or else jumping in the hair pile at Al Rosen the barber, both just a block from the house. But of course when they were able to hitch a truck it could take Mulcahey a whole day or even more before he brought them back. And when it was a garbage truck, generally he'd refuse.

Well, Ma saw there was no way to keep Nettie and Gittel locked up so instead she made Jonathan take them for an outing every day which you'll agree was only fair. I mean if not for *him*, that petty larceny prick, we wouldn't have *them*.

So Jonathan would shlep them around town on a Flexible Flyer from breakfast till 6 P.M. which of course they loved. Then he'd bring them home for supper, and that's when the trouble began. Naturally the old goers wanted to go again, but who could take them? Jonathan was too pooped from dragging the sled, and Libbie was too pooped from working all day at Monkey Ward. I had to be at my job at the Fine Arts Theatre. Pa can't go out in the dark because he gets lost. And Ma wouldn't leave the radio.

So at first Ma tried putting Nettie and Gittel to sleep right after supper. Incidentally, if you're wondering where they slept, here's the arrangement: Ma borrowed a crib from Mrs. Jorgensen over on Dayton Avenue. There was always a crib or two at the Jorgensens because they had this daughter Reba, about twenty-five years old with hot pants, who was all the time getting knocked up. Mr. Jorgensen, Reba's father, was assistant principal over at John Marshall Junior High and of course in his position he couldn't afford any scandals. So whenever Reba had a baby, they'd claim it was Mrs. Jorgensen's, not Reba's, and they'd raise the baby like their own.

There were six kids at the Jorgensen house, all ringers but Reba, and frankly I don't know who Mr. and Mrs. Jorgensen thought they were fooling. Maybe at first they could get away with it, but in my opinion it's not even worth trying once a woman passes seventy.

Anyhow Ma borrowed this crib from Mrs. Jorgensen which she set up in her bedroom, and that's where she put Nettie and Gittel to bed right after supper. They seemed willing enough. Ma undressed them, stuck them in the crib, gave them their good night treat—a piece of halvah for each—then kissed them and switched off the light. Sure enough, they were asleep in ten seconds.

So Ma went back to the living room and turned on Cecil B. deMille Presents The Lux Radio Theatre and about a half an hour later she was sitting there enjoying when—bang!—all of a sudden in ran Nettie and Gittel all dressed up and hollering for breakfast. Because that's what Ma didn't know yet: thirty minutes sleep per day was all they ever needed and they woke up refreshed like lions.

So we learned the bitter truth in a hurry: that from now on, every night and all night, Nettie and Gittel would be chasing each other through the house, bumping and thumping and hollering and banging the cymbals they stole from Ralph Rifkin, and nobody in the family would ever get a minute's sleep till I raised $200 to stick the old ladies in the Jewish Home for the Aged and Infirm.

Which of course meant marrying Celeste because where else would I get the money? Not from my salary at the Fine Arts Theatre, I can tell you. You know what that sonofabitch Zimmerman finally decided to pay me? *Fifteen cents an hour*, for Christ sakes!

"Mr. Zimmerman," I said to him on my first payday, "this is illegal under the Wagner Act."

"So go work for Wagner," he told me.

So all I could do was keep pressuring Celeste to set a wedding date. But go pressure Celeste. Believe me, it's easier to shit a football. Night after night I put the question to her, and night after night all she ever said was the same thing: "Oh, stop pestering and let's you-know." More and more I began to wonder if Jonathan hadn't been right when he told me I was out of my class tangling with millionaires. I mean, look at the score so far: A. M. Zimmerman had himself a doorman for fifteen cents an hour, and Celeste had herself a stud for free. And what did I have? A bent putz and two crazy boarders.

Meanwhile time kept flying. First November went, then December went, then 1937 was declared, and still I had no progress. And as if this wasn't discouragement enough, pretty soon I started getting needles at home from Kaplan, the King of Krime. "Nu, Baron Rothschild?" he'd say to me every night when I came in.

"Don't you worry," I'd say, forcing a smile and a wink and walking around whistling, he shouldn't know how bad things were.

But by the middle of January I couldn't keep up this shallow pretense no more. "Jonathan," I said, "I think I'm fucked."

"Well, Morris," he said, "I won't say I told you so."

"Good," I said. "Then I won't break your big oily nose."

"Because this is no time for I-told-you-so's," he said. "Kid, we got here a crisis. Have you taken a good look at your mother lately?"

"What about her?" I said.

"You know I ain't exactly ga-ga over the old hatchet," he said. "But still and all, it's no fun watching a person crumble up right in front of your eyes like *Lost Horizon*."

I stuck my head in the other room where Ma was sitting by the radio. She *did* look horseshit. She was shlumped in her chair fast asleep giving little moans

and twitches and mind you, the radio was playing real
loud—in fact, "Mary Noble, Backstage Wife," Ma's second
or third best favorite. And to show you how pooped Ma
was, not only was the radio blasting away but there
were terrible screams coming from the bathroom where
Nettie and Gittel was soaking in the tub. The old ladies
weren't screaming; they loved their bath. But the cat
didn't, so it was him.

But noise or not, Ma slept. So did everybody else in
fact. Pa was snoring at the breakfast table with his necktie in the farina. Libbie was at the sink washing dishes,
but not really. She was just holding a plate and sleeping
on her feet while the water ran.

"See, Morris?" said Jonathan. "Your own family—zom-
bies? Will you stop dreaming already about the Zimmerman millions and go call Ruthie Bumgarten?"

"I'll think about it," I said, and I really did because at
this point I would have taken help from anywheres. I
mean, the best I could save out of Zimmerman's coolie
wages was a crappy two dollars a week. So far all I'd
been able to stash away was twenty dollars and fifty
cents—the fifty cents was my Christmas bonus—So at
this rate it would take another ninety weeks before I
had enough to stick Nettie and Gittel in the Home. Who
could live so long? Besides Nettie and Gittel, I mean.

But then to my big surprise all of a sudden God took
a hand, or at least one of His partners did. What happened was I was standing at the Fine Arts Theatre taking
tickets one night when who should walk into the lobby
but none other than Sister Mary Frances of all people!
Well, this startled me, you can be sure, because we were

showing *Ecstasy* tonight which is pretty hot stuff, especially for nuns. There's one scene—a little bit out of focus, it's true—but Hedy Lamarr's ass is buck naked, no question.

"Hello, Sister," I said to Sister Mary Frances. "I think you got the wrong night. *Sign of the Cross* starts Friday."

"I've not come for the pictures, you ninny," she said. "'Tis you I've been trackin' down all day."

"What for?" I said.

"Can we go some place and talk?" she said.

"I can't leave my post," I said.

"Ask that young man there to take over for a minute," she said.

"He can't leave the popcorn machine," I said.

"Not even for a minute?" she said.

"Listen," I said, "Mr. Zimmerman once fired a guy for bending down to tie his shoe."

"Very well, we'll talk right here," she said. "It's about Bridget."

"Oh, my God!" I hollered. "Something happened to her?"

"You still love her then?" said Sister Mary Frances.

"Does Heinz still make pickles?" I said.

"Then you must get her back," she said.

"I can't," I said.

"Yes, yes, I'm quite aware you don't know how to write poems," she said. "But write one anyhow. I don't mean a jape like that last abomination you tried. Don't steal this time, Morris. Write your *own* abomination. I assure you, it won't matter how wretched."

"For your information," I said, getting my dander up a

little bit, "it so happens that I have recently finished a new poem which in my opinion is one of the real, true greats."

"Oh, bushwa!" she said. "But as I say, it won't matter. Bridget knows nothin' about poetry, the sweet little addlepate."

"She *don't?*" I said.

"Never has," said Sister Mary Frances. "Oh, sure, her head's full of it, but she likes it *all*, the dear dolt—Henley, Joaquin Miller, Edgar Guest, even that Jezebel, Edna Millay. You've nothin' to worry about, Morris. Give her your dreary poem."

"Listen," I said, "how come you're so hot to get me and Bridget back together?"

"Because she's publishing the banns next Sunday," she said.

"I don't like the sound of that," I said. "What does it mean?"

"She's announcing her engagement to Bruce Albright," she said.

"Oh, no!" I hollered.

"You can't let her do it," said Sister Mary Frances, grabbing my sleeve. "She doesn't love Bruce and never will."

"So what's she banning him for?" I said.

"Because she hasn't the strength left to resist," she said. "She's faint with love of you and sick with the futility of it. Give her your poem, my son."

"I wish I could," I said.

"Why can't you, for pity's sake?" she said.

"It's too hard to exp—" I started to say but then I

stopped dead. Because at this very moment, who should be walking into the outer lobby but A. M. Zimmerman himself! That's all I needed—Zimmerman should find out about me and Bridget!

"Good evening, Mr. Zimmerman," I said.

"Never mind good evening," he said. "How long has this nun been hanging around?"

"Just a couple minutes," I said.

"Enough already," he said. "Sister, here's a quarter and good-by."

"Thank you, sir," she said. "I'll put it in our Angelus bell repair fund."

"I don't care if you put it in your wimple," he said. "But scram, will you? It's terrible for business, nuns mooching in the lobby."

"Directly, sir, directly," she said.

"Morris," he said, "did you get the urinal unplugged?"

"Yeah," I said. "It was a teddy bear."

"Fucking kiddie matinees," he said. "Excuse my French, Sister, but what are you hanging around for? Do I hang around the convent?"

"I'll be goin', sir, and ever so gladly, but first I'll conclude my business," she said.

"What kind of business you got with Morris?" he said.

"The Angelus bell repair fund," I said.

"From *him* you want money?" he said. "That's rich."

"So when you gonna give me a raise?" I said.

"The twenty-third of Never," he said. "How's the house tonight?"

"Packed," I said.

"It better be," he said. "You know how much I took in here last night? Eleven dollars!"

"So who told you to book Bobby Breen in *Hawaii Calls?*" I said.

"You're right," he said. "How drunk is the projectionist?"

"Staggering a little bit," I said, "but he got the reels in the right order this time."

"Fucking unions," he said. "Excuse me, Sister. You still hanging around? Well, I'm not. Good-by. Turn down the thermostat, Morris. I'm not running no Turkish bath here."

"Okay," I said and pushed the thermostat down from sixty-two to fifty-eight while Zimmerman went off to cheer up some more employees.

Sister Mary Frances stood there looking after Zimmerman and crossing herself, fifty or sixty times maybe, and then she turned back to me. "If I happen to hear of another job, Morris, I'll keep you in mind," she said.

"I'd appreciate," I said.

"Now then, about Bridget," she said. "You must give her your poem, my son."

"I can't, I tell you," I said.

"You *must!*" she hollered. "It's God's will! A romance this inscrutable could be nothin' else."

"God, schmod," I said. "I need *money.*"

"Oh, my poor Bridget fallen among Hebrews!" she hollered.

"What are you hollering?" I said. "You're so anxious to get me back with Bridget? Okay, lend me some money."

"Me?" she said. "I've taken a vow of poverty."

"That was a crazy thing to do," I said. "How about the rest of your outfit?"

"Everybody," she said.

"Oh, come on," I said, giving her a nudge. "Somebody over there must have a few bucks squirreled away."

"Morris," she said, "speaking as treasuress, I can assure you that our entire liquidity consists of one hundred and fifty-eight dollars painfully mooched coin by coin to repair the Angelus bell."

"Wait a minute," I said, getting excited. Because all of a sudden I saw a way out. Two hundred dollars I needed. Twenty I already saved up. If I could get another 158 from the nun, I'd only be shy 22, and that much I could save in eleven more weeks. Ma could live that long probably.

Of course, she might topple over dead when I told her about Bridget, but that didn't seem too likely. Jewish mothers do very little actual dying from shicksas. A lots of hemorrhaging, of course. But actual dying is seldom.

And besides, I wouldn't tell Ma about Bridget till *after* I got rid of Nettie and Gittel. That ought to make it go down a little easier. So wasn't it worth a gamble? Celeste was up the spout anyways, that was clear, so why shouldn't I have a little happiness at least from the girl I loved and adored, Bridget?

"Sister," I said to Sister Mary Frances, "tell you what I'm gonna do: Lend me the 158 and I'll take Bridget back."

"I certainly will not!" she said. "The very idea!"

"Okay, okay, don't lend it to me," I said. "Some day I

hope you'll tell Bridget you loved a bell better than her."

"Oh, you devil," said Sister Mary Frances. Then she thought for a while, yanking her beads and pacing back and forth in her Ground Grippers. "All right," she said at last, "God forgive me but I'm goin' to do it."

"Now you're talking," I said. "How soon can I have the money?"

"As soon as you publish *your* banns with Bridget," she said.

"Couldn't I have it a little sooner?" I said.

"Not one second sooner, you deicide," she said.

"Well, okay," I said, and a few hours later after giving Celeste her nightly diddle, I went home to dig out my great translation of Itzik Fishel's *Esther Resnick, American* from the drawer where I hid it. Naturally it wasn't there. Since Nettie and Gittel, nothing was ever where you hid it. In the last week alone Pa's tallis and Libbie's diaphragm had both disappeared.

But I got a good memory as it happens, so I was able to recall the entire poem. I wrote it down and the first thing next morning I brought it to Bridget.

Chapter Sixteen

I'm not going to stall around and keep you in suspense.
I'll tell you right away that Bridget loved the new poem.

Did she love it because it was true what Sister Mary
Frances said: that Bridget wouldn't know a good poem
if it bit her in the ass? Or did she love it because it
happened to be one of the real true greats? Well, you
know what I think but don't let that influence you. Here's
the poem and you make up your own mind. I'm confident
you'll come to a fair decision, no matter what snotty re-
marks you might have heard from nuns.

ESTHER RESNICK, AMERICAN
Last night a girl aged sixteen years,
Named Esther Resnick, not J. P. Morgan,
Took out her pair of pinking shears,
And plunged them through a vital organ.

Why did this lassie die so young?
Why lays she now in death's cold rigor,
With her eyes-a-glazed and her fair pink tongue,
A-turning black and a-getting bigger?

She was just an innocent immigrant maid,
Who came from Poland, shy and green,
And found a job in the garment trade,
By the menswear factory of Meyer Levine.

Levine was a typical capitalist swine,
If you joined the union, he gave you the boot,
If you went to the toilet, he docked you a dime,
If you died, he repossessed your suit.

Poor Esther slaved in his cutting room,
Toiling long hours and sweating quarts,
Yet who can tell where love will bloom?
'Twas here she met young Irving Schwartz.

Irving worked across the table,
To a cutter he was apprenticed,
An ambitious lad and very able,
He studied nights to be a dentist.

But it wasn't to be, this tender romance,
For Meyer Levine like a typical boss,
One day called in Esther, unbuttoned his pants,
And told her, "You're fired if you don't come across."

"Oh, no!" she shrieked. "I am marrying soon!
Don't make me unfit to wear a white dress!
The wedding is set for the twelfth of June,
When Irving is getting his D.D.S."

She fell on her knees and begged for her virtue,
But Levine, he only gave a shrug.
"Come on," he said, "it wouldn't hurt you."
And he wreaked his will on the office rug.

Well, that's how it is in the U.S.A.
A working girl don't find gold in the street.
Disgrace she finds and a twelve-hour day,
And the boss on her belly if she wants to eat.

So Esther that night her quietus made,
Who never knew joy or anything near it.
Tomorrow her last remains get laid.
Rest, Esther. Rest, perturbèd spirit.

So comrades from the garment trade,
Learn something from this grim charade:
Don't ever trust a boss's promise,
And next time vote for Norman Thomas.

"Oh, Morris, it's a marvelous poem!" hollered Bridget. "But it is more than just a poem. It is the wild keening of an outraged heart. How wise you were not to polish."

"Thanks," I said, giving a modest smile.

"How *apt*, this clumsiness!" she said. "How deeply, deeply human!"

"I try my best, is all," I said.

"I do hope you'll write some more in this gauche new vein," she said.

"Sure thing," I said. "Every Sunday if you want."

"Oh, Morris, Morris!" she said. "To think I ever doubted you!"

"That's okay," I said. "We all make mistakes."

"How Jewish of you to forgive," she said.

"When you gonna dump Bruce Albright?" I said.

"As soon as you say you'll have me back," she said.

"I'll have you back," I said.

"I love you," she said.

"And I love you," I said and gave her a kiss right in the *L'Etoile du Nord.*

"Not here, sweet eaglet," she said. "Someone might see."

"Who?" I said.

"Us!" hollered Lance Berman and Claude Applebaum who were up in the transom giggling.

"Let's wait till tonight, dear Morris," said Bridget.

"Well, here's the thing," I said. "I'm working nights at the theater, so for a while I'm afraid I can only see you in the daytime."

"Not for long, I hope," she said.

"Not too," I said. "Just eleven weeks."

"Oh, Morris," she hollered, "it is just as I feared! You *have* stopped loving me, haven't you?"

"I love you, I love you," I said. "Keep your shirt on."

"Oh, thank God!" she said and gave me another kiss, but naturally not much of a one with Lance and Claude snickering in the transom.

"Let's go someplace where we can be alone," I said.

"Gladly, dear minstrel," she said.

So we went out and started looking. But where can you find privacy in the daytime? I mean *real* privacy—somewheres I could hold Bridget and kiss her and smell her hair again. And also—I'm going to level with you—to do intercourse on her if she seemed willing, which I felt sure she'd seem. Because I'd made up my mind not to be a schmuck like I was the last time—letting Bridget get away because I was waiting for the perfect time and place to do it. I'd learned my lesson, believe me: when it comes to humping, the perfect time is *now* and the perfect place is the nearest flat surface.

But, as I say, where can you do it in the daytime where you won't get arrested? The River Bank was definitely out and so was the stadium. A hotel room would have been fine of course, if I had the money which I didn't. Or if I could have borrowed a car I might have found a culvert or somewheres safe to park, but who'd lend me a car? Not Celeste, you can be sure, and not my cousin

Albert either because he was driving around looking for work all day. He wasn't in school any more. When Aunt Lena found out about the fur coat, she dis-enrolled him the very next day so she could get his tuition back—which, incidentally, was far from easy. The bursar told Aunt Lena there were positively no refunds after six weeks, but she stood in front of his window screaming, "Antisemite!" till he finally broke down. Three and a half days it took, and the money finally came out of the bursar's own pocket, the poor bastard.

Incidentally, while I'm talking about Albert—or Mr. Tough Titty as I was starting in to call him because that's the kind of luck he had—let me tell you the latest. Being out of school now and naturally finding no jobs, Albert decided he might as well enter some of those contests you see in the newspaper. You know: Find all the Oxydol boxes concealed in this picture and then complete this sentence in twenty-five words or less: I like Oxydol because . . .

Well, you know what kind of thoroughness Albert got. He didn't just enter *some* contests; he entered every one on every page of the paper, even the ones on the kiddies page, so wouldn't you know it? That's what he finally won: a kiddie contest. I hate to tell you the prize: a Shetland pony. *Alive,* I mean.

"Don't worry, I'll sell it," he told Aunt Lena. So he went out and tried and he learned something: if there's one item that nobody in the whole St. Paul wants including the humane society, it's a Shetland pony. And it wasn't even kosher so you could eat it.

So Albert put it the only place he could—down the

cellar—and Aunt Lena had another topic to scream about besides the fur coat. Also the horse wasn't too happy in the cellar so he kicked over the furnace, and now the whole family was going around the house in overcoats. You see what I mean about Mr. Tough Titty?

But back to Bridget, we wandered around campus looking for places to be private but there weren't any. So finally I let her shlep me into the University museum. It was that or freeze to death.

I almost wished I'd chose freezing. Not only did the museum have guards in every room to prevent grabass, but also there was an exhibit of somebody called Chagall who paints very Jewish so naturally Bridget went off her noodle from happiness. I thought sure she was going to break into a hora any minute. But she didn't. All she did was keep hollering stuff like "Such merry pathos!" and "Such pathetic merriment!"

"You bet," I kept answering but frankly by me pictures of flying rabbis is no way to kill an afternoon.

So I had plenty pathos myself when I brought Bridget back to her dorm around five-thirty. "Would you like to sit in the lobby and talk for a while?" she said.

"No," I said because this happened to be the one activity I wasn't too crazy about doing with Bridget: talking. "I don't suppose I could come up to your room for a minute," I said.

"You don't suppose correct, buster," said the house mother.

"Good night, Morris. I love you," said Bridget, holding Vachel Lindsay's *Song Bag* in front of her face so the house mother couldn't lip-read.

"I love you too," I said which I certainly did, even if this reunion so far was a real glass of shit.

"Good night, my eaglet," she said.

"Listen," I said, ducking behind the Vachel Lindsay, "you wouldn't happen to know anyone who got an apartment within walking distance?"

"I'm afraid not," she said.

"How about within *streetcar* distance?" I said.

"Oh, my beloved," she said, "don't you think that I too am burning to hold you in my arms?"

"Burning, eh?" I said.

"Aflame," she said. "To cleave, to meld, to become as one."

"Do you know anybody with a *garage* maybe?" I said.

"No," she said. "Can't you get a night off soon?"

"No," I said.

"Oh, well, at least we still have our afternoons," she said. "And there's all kinds of marvelous things coming up—the Maxfield Parrish retrospective, the Flemish altar cloth exhibit—oh, lots and lots of things."

"Maybe I can," I said.

"Get a night off?" she said.

"I'll find out," I said.

Chapter Seventeen

I tried. Naturally I knew better than to ask Zimmerman so I worked on Celeste instead.

"Celeste," I said to her that night when the hump was over and I was helping her look for her barrette, "do you think you could get your father to give me the night off tomorrow?"

"What for?" she said.

"My Uncle Nochim is coming in from Duluth," I said. "I didn't see him for ten years already."

"A likely story," she said. "You got another girl again, don't you?"

"What a silly idea, my darling," I said, giving this little tinkly laugh.

"You must have," said Celeste. "The whole night you didn't pester me to get married."

"Okay, let's get married," I said.

"Stop pestering," she said.

"So how's about tomorrow night off?" I said.

"No," she said. "You can see this alleged uncle in the morning."

"He's catching the midnight train for Chicago," I said.

"Why didn't you say so?" she said. "Okay, I'll fix it with Daddy."

"You mean it?" I said.

"Why, sure," she said. "And by the way, I'm coming along to meet this uncle."

"Now just a minute," I said.

"Ha-ha, the joke's on you," she said. "You want to try again?"

"Okay, I guess I'll have to tell you the real reason," I said.

"Oh, boy, this should be great," she said.

"I got to have a tumor operated," I said.

"Good going, Morris!" she said. "That's the way to lie— *big!*"

"I only wish I was," I said.

"Where have you got this alleged tumor?" she said.

"That's just it," I said. "It keeps moving."

"Where is it now roughly?" she said. "I'd like a feel."

"How would you like this barrette up your nose?" I said.

"How would you like to work tomorrow night?" said Celeste.

And that finished that.

So I knew there'd be no nights with Bridget, only those long humpless afternoons at the museum. Naturally I kept looking for someplace where you could do daytime boffing but it was no use. I did have one fairly good idea—a furniture store on a slow Monday—but I finally decided against it. Just as well, probably.

Well, as you can see, things weren't too great, but on the other hand they weren't too desperate either. Until one morning I came to school and found a note in my P.O. box from Mr. Harwood telling me to report to his

office. Right away I felt a chill grab a hold of my heart
because what did I ever get from Mr. Harwood except
bad news, that prick?

As I walked into his office I saw a copy of *Esther
Resnick, American* laying on his desk, so I figured that
must be the bad news: he wasn't going to let Bridget
publish the poem because it was too sexy or too communist or too both. To tell you the truth, I didn't care a
whole lot. After all, the poem had done its job—getting
Bridget back—so why kick?

"Okay, so you won't let the poem get published, right?"
I said to Mr. Harwood.

"Correct," he said. "But there's a bit more. Sit down,
please, Mr. Katz."

Then he surprised me: he gave me a smile—a squeaky
little thing, it's true, but still the first one I ever saw on
that pinchy face of his. So I sat down and he not only
surprised me again, but he damn near put me six feet
under. Listen to what he said:

"Momser," he said, "why are you plagiarizing Itzik
Fishel?"

"Oh, no!" I hollered and for a second everything went
black and the room started in whirling around. This
couldn't be happening, it just *couldn't!* "Oh, no!" I hollered. "You're not *Jewish?*"

"Nu, why not?" he said.

"How does a Jew get a name Harwood?" I said.

"One starts with Horowitz," he said. "But shall we
return to your plagiarism?"

"Stop calling it plagiarism," I said.

"What do *you* call it?" he said.

"Plagiarism is stealing," I said. "I didn't *steal*. Believe me, I worked a hell of a lot harder on that poem than Fishel ever did."

"A novel interpretation," he said. "I wonder how the Dean will like it."

"Wait a minute," I said, starting in to shake. "You told this to the *Dean?*" Because if the Dean knew, everybody else would, especially Bridget. Then I'd be absolutely a goner.

"Not yet, but of course I'm going to," said Mr. Harwood.

"Don't," I said. "Let me explain what happened."

"I'm sure it would be endlessly diverting," he said. "But I have a class in thirty minutes."

"I'll just hit the high spots," I said.

So I told him a condensed but still heartbreaking version of what had been going on with Bridget, Celeste, Crip, Albert, Ma, Jonathan, and Nettie and Gittel.

"Well, that's about it, Mr. Harwood," I said when I finished. "And I certainly hope you got a fuller understanding now."

"I have indeed, Mr. Katz," he said, "and I sympathize profoundly."

"So how come you're laughing?" I said because all of a sudden he started. He tried not to, but snorts and wheezes kept spurting out and his glasses fogged up so bad he had to take them off and wipe them about thirty times.

"Hey, listen," I said to him, "you want a *real* laugh? I got some pictures of the *Morro Castle* going down."

"I'm sorry, Mr. Katz," he said, finally getting control of himself. "I *do* sympathize, I assure you."

"Tell it to Sweeney," I said.

"No, it's true," he said. "I know this will require rather a large suspension of disbelief on your part, but long, long ago I too was a player in this same forlorn comedy."

My jaw dropped open. "You mean you fell in love with a shicksa?" I said.

"Hard to credit, isn't it?" he said.

"You're not kidding," I said. "How serious was it?"

"I got my nose fixed," he said. "Does that give you an indication?"

"Yes," I said. "A beautiful job, by the way."

"You really think so?" he said.

"It fooled *me*," I said. "But what happened with the shicksa?"

"What always happens?" he said.

"Your mother?" I said.

"What then?" he said. "And how do you propose to deal with yours?"

"Damned if I know," I said. "How did you deal with yours?"

"I waited for her to die," he said.

"How long did it take?" I said.

"Don't be silly," he said. "She's still alive. The shicksa is dead though."

"Well, it probably wouldn't have helped anyhow if your mother croaked," I said. "From what I hear, even if they go they leave a curse."

"That's my understanding," he said. "Then why do you persist, Mr. Katz?"

"Love," I said. "I can't go on without Bridget. Are you gonna help me or not?"

"Not," he said.

"A prick to the end," I said.

"I can't," he said.

"Yes, you can," I said. "You know why? Because if you don't, I'm gonna tell the whole University you're a Jew."

"You're a hard man, Katz," he said.

"It's a hard world, Horowitz," I said.

"However, they already know I'm a Jew," he said. "Why do you suppose I haven't had a promotion in twelve years?"

"Looks like I'm screwed," I said.

"You should be," he said. "And royally. I can't think why I'm letting you off."

My jaw dropped open again. "You *are?*" I said.

"I am myself amazed, Mr. Katz," he said. "It's best you go quickly."

"Not till I say thanks," I said. "Thanks, Mr. Harwood, and I want you to know you'll always be aces in my deck."

"No fawning," he said. "Go now and plagiarize no more."

"Why not?" I said. "You won't let the poems get published anyhow and meanwhile I'll keep Bridget happy. So who's hurt?"

"Will you take your chutzpah and go already?" he said.

"Right away," I said. "Let me ask you one question: You wouldn't have an apartment I could use this afternoon?"

"The Dean has a nicer one," he said. "Shall I call him?"

"I'm going," I said.

"Shalom," he said.

So I went and took Bridget to a pewter exhibit.

Chapter Eighteen

For the whole eleven weeks I never did find a location for afternoon poon with Bridget, so it was the same damn museum day after day. It might have been a little better if there were a few other museums on campus but there weren't and, believe me, once you have seen the Laocoön 77 times you don't care if you never see another marble asshole as long as you live.

Even Bridget began to fidget after a couple weeks so I translated another Itzik Fishel to quieten her down. This new one was greater even than *Esther Resnick, American* in my opinion which I hope you've come to have a little respect for by this time. It was called *The Great Triangle Shirtwaist Company Fire* and it was about this famous sweatshop fire in New York back around 1911 which you probably heard of, where 146 Jewish and Italian immigrant girls got burned to death because the cheap, chiseling boss had never put in any fire escapes; instead he slipped the cops a few bucks not to report him.

You already know what the combination of me and Itzik Fishel is like, so there's no need giving you the whole poem. But you might enjoy a little sample, so

here's the first stanza. If you're not interested, just skip
over.

> *A hundred and forty-six girls are dead,*
> *A curse should be on the boss's head,*
> *'Twas him together with crooked cops,*
> *Who killed those innocent Jews and wops.*

The rest, if I may say so, was in the same general
quality. In fact, Bridget thought it was far superior. I
don't know what Mr. Harwood thought. He got to
laughing so hard, the prick, that I had to thump him on
the back he shouldn't choke. Well, you know Mr. Harwood.

Anyhow, the eleven weeks went crawling by somehow,
and the Nettie-Gittel removal fund kept ootzing ahead
little by little. Naturally we'd have all liked the fund to
grow faster, not just me and my family, but all the
neighbors too, because by now the whole Selby Avenue
was starting in to cuss and mutter about the old ladies.
What made everybody so sore was this new stunt Nettie
and Gittel thought up lately: they'd go around stealing
clotheslines which they'd cut into six-foot jump ropes
and then trade them to the kids at Webster Elementary
School for their lunch. So everybody was bitching—
the former clothesline owners and the kids' mothers too.

Well, finally came March 21, the first day of spring no
matter what the thermometer said—it said eight below—
but in my heart it was green and sunny because for me
the eleven weeks were finally over at last. Tonight I was
going to give Celeste her walking papers, and tomorrow
would start a wonderful new life: no more Celeste, no

more A. M. Zimmerman, no more Nettie and Gittel. Instead there'd be me and Bridget and true happiness at last, except of course my mother.

So I never stopped grinning and smiling the whole day long, right up until 11 P.M. when Celeste parked her Olds in front of the Fine Arts Theatre to pick me up as usual. That's when I stopped grinning and smiling because to tell you the truth it made me a little sad all of a sudden, knowing I was about to give Celeste her walking papers. Not sad because this crotch-busting affair was finally over thank God, but sad because when you came right down to it, Celeste was not a *bad* person, just piggy and ruthless, and I really didn't have any grudges against her. So I made up my mind to let her down as easy as I could, even throw in a farewell hump if she wasn't crying too hard.

I started to get in the Olds but something was funny: Celeste didn't slide over to let me drive like she always did. She stayed behind the wheel. "Get in the other side," she said.

I did. "How come you're driving?" I said.

"Nobody's driving. We're staying right here," she said.

"We can't you-know *here*," I said. "A streetcar goes by every twenty minutes."

"Morris, I got something to tell you," she said.

"Isn't that funny? I got something to tell you too," I said.

"Ladies first," she said.

"Okay, shoot," I said.

"I love you, Morris," she said.

"I'll be a sonofabitch!" I said, giving a jump. "When did you find out?"

"This afternoon," she said.

"I didn't see you this afternoon," I said.

"I know," she said. "I kept ducking behind statues."

"You *followed* me?" I hollered.

"Stop hollering," she said. "I know you got another girl. I just wanted to take a look."

"She's only a casual acquaintance, is all," I said. (You see how a person gets into habits? Why was I still lying to Celeste?)

"You know what I was going to do tonight, Morris?" said Celeste.

"What?" I said.

"I was going to ask you to take a look at my front tire and then run you over," she said.

"I'm glad you changed your mind," I said.

"Yes," she said. "That's no kind of a way to hold a boy."

"I agree a hundred per cent," I said.

"The best thing is to dump you," she said. "So this is it, Morris. You're all washed up."

"Now just a minute!" I hollered. "Just a darn minute! Are you gonna dump the man you love just because you got a little jealous?" (Now you go figure that one! What was I arguing for? Wasn't the whole idea to finish up this thing with Celeste? And wasn't it getting finished? So what did it matter who dumped who? But it *did* matter. Don't ask me why.)

"You're wrong, Morris," she said. "I didn't get a *little* jealous. I got a *lot* jealous. In fact, my first idea was to run *her* over."

"Celeste!" I said, giving a gasp.

"It's the truth," she said. "That's why I got to dump you, Morris, before I kill somebody. This is making me very nervous, these big emotions. I mean what's the use of money if you can't behave with refined quietness?"

"I hope you realize you're never gonna find another guy," I said. (You see? Still arguing.)

"Oh, I don't know," she said. "Luckily there's a Depression, thank God, so there's got to be more fortune hunters around."

"Maybe so, but you won't find one you love," I said. (Why couldn't I stop arguing, for Christ sakes?)

"That suits me fine," she said. "Who wants to love somebody who don't love them back? What kind of a bargaining position is that?"

"What if he *does* love you back?" I said.

"Ho-ho-ho," she said. "Well, good-by, Morris. You want to shake?"

I didn't but I did anyhow.

"Hey, I nearly forgot. Don't you have something to tell me too?" she said.

"Not any more," I said.

"Well, good-by then," she said. "Oh, listen, you wouldn't happen to know of any boys I might look into?"

"As a matter of fact, yes," I said. "Lance Berman and Claude Applebaum."

"Thanks," she said. "Oh, by the way, Daddy says to tell you you're fired. Good-by, Morris."

"Good-by, Celeste," I said and went home to get all the sleep I could because tomorrow I was starting this wonderful new life.

Chapter Nineteen

I didn't sleep at all, not one wink, and it wasn't Nettie and Gittel's fault this time. You know what kept me awake? I couldn't stop thinking about Celeste. How do you like that? I wanted her back. Really; I'm not kidding. I wanted her back not to *keep* her, God forbid. I wanted her back so this time *I* could do the dumping. That's what was puckering my ass: that *she* should have handed out the walking papers, not me. So the whole night long I kept trying to think up schemes to trap her again.

Did you ever hear anything so stupid? If I couldn't sleep why didn't I at least lay there and kvell about how glorious things were going to be from now on with my beautiful, tender-hearted, sweet-natured Bridget? Why couldn't I do anything except brood about how to get back a mean, homely broad whose idea of a lovers' quarrel was to run you over with a car?

But morning finally came and I got a hold of myself and said, Okay, dummy, enough dumbness, there's work to be done. The first order of business was to go see my cousin Albert and get him to lend me his car for tonight because that was the next order of business: to have a date with Bridget in the darkness at last, give her a nice boff, and then propose to her so I could get the

$158 from Sister Mary Frances and complete the Nettie-Gittel removal fund.

Well, imagine my surprise as I walked up to Albert's house and there was Albert outside by the curb trying to tie the Shetland pony onto the fender of his car!

"Hey, Morris, hold the sonofabitch's hind legs, will you?" he said.

"Albert," I said, "why are you tying the horse on your fender?"

"Because I can't get the sonofabitch to fit inside," he said.

"That still don't answer my question," I said.

"I got good news," said Albert, looking all gleamy-eyed like he does when he gets excited. "Hold the hind legs and I'll tell you."

So I did and he told me the good news: he'd been hanging around Di Palma's produce house yesterday and he happened to hear about this farmer up near Brainerd, Minnesota, who had a big farm and a lots of kids and he was in the market for a Shetland pony. So that's where Albert was taking the horse.

"Well, Albert, I'm very happy for you," I said. "How far is Brainerd?"

"A hundred and twenty miles," he said.

"So you'll be back tonight?" I said.

"Sure," he said. "You want to come along for the ride?"

"I don't mind," I said. "But I need to borrow your car when we get back."

"Nothing doing," he said. "You're after this Bridget cooz again, ain't you?"

"Yes, and I better get her this time," I said and told him why.

"Well, Morris," he said when I finished, "if that's how it is, then that's how it is. How you gonna break it to your mother?"

"I don't know yet," I said. "Telegram probably."

"Yes, that's the best," he said and finished tying the horse to the fender and off we drove.

The trip passed very nicely with good conversation and friendly laughing. Then we got to Brainerd and the laughing ended for the day. In fact, in Albert's case, it ended for *twenty* days, still another bad break for this truly unfortunate human being.

What happened was we drove into Brainerd and Albert pulled up to this cop who was standing on the corner. "Officer," said Albert, "would you know a farmer around here called Holmquist?"

"Why, sure," said the cop.

"Great," said Albert. "Would you know if he's in the market for a Shetland pony?"

"That there is true," said the cop.

"Great," said Albert again. "Would you know how I get to his farm?"

"Is that there the animal you want to sell?" said the cop, pointing at Albert's fender.

"Ain't he a pip?" said Albert.

"Son," said the cop, "that there animal is froze."

"To death?" said Albert.

"That there is my diagnosis," said the cop.

"No, it can't be," said Albert and he hopped out of the

car and tried artificial respiration for fifteen or twenty minutes. But the cop was right.

But that wasn't the worst of it. Here's the worst of it: "Was that there late animal ever vaccinated for hoof-and-mouth?" said the cop.

"How the fuck would I know?" said Albert.

"Then according to Ordinance 22b he got to be buried before sundown on the day of his deceasal," said the cop.

So he showed us this field outside of town, and Albert and me started digging with all our might—and I don't have to tell you what Albert's might is like—but it didn't help. All afternoon we hacked away and didn't make a dent in that frozen ground, not even with a crowbar.

Meanwhile it was getting on toward sunset so the cop finally sent for a steam shovel. That did the trick all right, but then the cop handed Albert the bill— *twenty dollars* for Christ sakes!

"I ain't got twenty dollars!" Albert hollered. "I ain't got twenty *cents*."

"You got twenty *days?*" said the cop.

"You gonna stick me in the workhouse?" said Albert.

"Not me," said the cop. "The judge."

"Listen, Officer," I said to the cop, "how's about making it *ten* days and we'll *both* go to the workhouse?"

"No, Morris, I can't let you," said Albert.

"Okay," I said because I wasn't all that crazy to do it anyhow.

"Take good care of my car," Albert said to me.

"I will," I said to him. "Keep smiling, kid."

Then I drove back to St. Paul wondering what tragedy would strike poor Albert next. I mean besides getting buggered in the Brainerd workhouse: with his luck that was the *least* that could happen.

Chapter Twenty

To tell you the truth, I wasn't specially in the mood to take Bridget out when I got back to St. Paul, what with being so depressed about Albert and still pissed off at Celeste. Still and all, Bridget was a marvelous girl who I loved and she'd been patient all these weeks and it really wouldn't be fair to make her keep on waiting. Besides the thing to do was get this business over with. The sooner my mother got told, the sooner she'd recover. If she was going to, that is.

So at eight o'clock I picked up Bridget in the lobby of the women's dorm and walked her out to the Maytag.

"Oh, Morris, look! A lover's moon!" said Bridget.

"Watch out for the manure on the running board," I said.

"How in the world did that get there?" she said.

"I just bought some gas from the Flying Red Horse," I said and started for the River Bank.

"Ah, my eaglet is joking," she said, giving a laugh. "Shall you be *L'Allegro* tonight, Morris?"

"Maybe yes," I said, "and maybe no."

"Or shall you be *Il Penseroso?*" she said.

"Who can tell?" I said, wishing we'd get to the River Bank already and stop this Choctaw.

"Be *L'Allegro*," she said.

"Whatever you say," I said.

"For this is a night of joy," she said. "What could be more joyful than to hold one another again at long last under a lover's moon?"

"Provided we find a place to park," I said because now we were at the River Bank and it was jammed with cars. Spring always brings out the humpers, even when it's cold enough to kill a horse as you know.

But I finally found a spot between two cars and parked and cut the motor and put my arm around Bridget and pulled her to me gently like I used to and smelled her hair. One thing about Bridget: I never hope to meet a girl with a better smelling head.

"How brightly she shines, Morris," said Bridget, pointing at the sky. Then she quoted some poetry, a habit I hoped to break her of before too long. *"The orbèd maiden with white fire laden,"* she quoted, *"whom mortals call the moon."*

But I wasn't looking at any orbèd maiden, I'll tell you that. I was looking at the car on my left. It was an Oldsmobile—like Celeste's—1936 model—like Celeste's— green colored—like Celeste's—with a squirrel tail on the antenna—like Celeste's—and there were two people screwing in the back seat.

I can't explain what came over me. It was like I turned into a mad, savage beast all of a sudden, I gave a roar and flang Bridget aside and jerked open my door and leapt out and raced to the Olds and jerked open *its* door. And, mind you, I was roaring all the time. Not words, just roaring.

But, believe me, I stopped roaring in a hurry once I opened up the Olds. Because it wasn't who I thought or anywheres near it. Actually it was Mr. Harwood banging the Homecoming Queen.

Well, in situations like this there's really nothing you can say that will put people at their ease, so I just mumbled a little small talk—I don't even remember what —something like, "Well, folks, is it cold enough for you?" Then I smiled and closed their door and went back to Bridget.

"A mistake," I told her. "I thought it was my Uncle Nochim from Duluth."

It took a little while to calm Bridget down because I'd made her pretty jumpy, but finally I got it done. Actually it was a lot harder to calm myself down, but finally I did that too. Meanwhile Mr. Harwood started the Olds and drove away, shaking his fist at me.

So Bridget and I sat for a half hour or so, calming down and waiting for the old feeling to take a hold. It got a hold on Bridget before me. "Eaglet, eaglet!" she kept saying and nuzzling me. "Oh, enter me, eaglet!"

And I'd have done it too because I was building a nice lump in my pants by now, but all of a sudden I saw another Oldsmobile pulling into the River Bank. This one parked a couple rows down, too far away to see the color, but I could tell it was a '36. And there was a squirrel tail hanging on the antenna, no question.

But this time I wasn't going to tear around like my ass was on fire. "Excuse me, Bridget," I said calmly. "I think I see my Uncle Nochim again."

"Eaglet, don't go!" she hollered. "Not *now* for God's love!"

"I shan't be a minute," I said.

Then I walked, not ran, to the Oldsmobile and I gently opened, not jerked, the back door.

Well, if you think I was sore the first time, you should have seen me now. *Berserk* is the closest word, and that isn't even close. I won't try to describe how it was because, to be honest, I hate to think about it even now. All I'll tell you is there was only one word in my mind —only one: KILL.

It was Celeste all right. And you know who was with her? *Henry Leibowitz!* Can you imagine such a thing? *Henry Leibowitz!*

"Morris, Morris, for God sakes, don't hit!" he hollered. "Look how little I am!"

"Get out of the car, you sonofabitch!" I said.

"It's not my fault, Morris," he hollered. "I'll prove it to you. Where's my pants?"

"Stand up and fight, you sneaky traitor," I said.

"Celeste, you seen my pants?" he said.

"Here," she said.

"Oh, thank God," he said and while I was trying to yank him out of the car, he managed to stick his hand in his pants pocket and fish out a note. "Look, Morris. It's not my fault, see?" he said, shoving me the note. "This was in my P.O. box this morning. Read it."

"After I kill you," I said.

"Now, please," he begged.

"Okay, but *then* I'll kill you," I said.

So I read the note and I quote:

Dear Henry,
I am the girl who sits behind you in Psych I,
not too pretty maybe but very well dressed. Would you
like to go to the movies tonight? I get in free and
I have my own car.

Sincerely,
Celeste Zimmerman

P.S. I put out.

"You see?" said Henry. "Not my fault. So don't hit, okay, Morris?"

"Okay," I said. "But get out of the car. I want to talk to Celeste private."

"I'll freeze my balls off out there," hollered Henry, but I pulled him out anyhow, got in myself, and closed the door.

"Well, Miss Zimmerman," I said, "I have heard of some pretty low tricks in my time."

"Me too," she said. "Like sending a girl to look up Lance Berman and Claude Applebaum."

"You went?" I said.

"Stop grinning, you cockaroach," she said.

"Serves you right," I said. "Now shut up. I'll do the talking."

"Who you telling shut up?" she said.

"*You,* satchel-ass. And I'll tell you somthing else too," I said. "The next time I catch you with another guy, I'll put the both of you in the hospital."

"Well, well, if it isn't Killer Katz, the Fighting Doorman," she said.

"I said shut up," I said. "From now on there's gonna

be respect and consideration. Let's get that straight right now before we're married."

"Before *who's* married?" she said.

"You heard me," I said. "You're gonna marry me and the discussion is closed."

"You're out of your head," she said.

"That would explain it," I said.

"What about your other girl?" she said.

"I'm glad you reminded me," I said and opened the car door. "Henry," I said, "come with me for a minute."

"Without *pants?*" said Henry.

"Sorry," I said. "Here you are."

So Henry put on the pants.

"I'll be right back," I said to Celeste.

"I won't be here," she said.

"I think you will," I said and took the car keys. "Come, Henry," I said and walked him over to the Maytag and opened the door.

"Bridget," I said, "I'm terrible sorry but we live in two different worlds and it never would have worked. Try and forgive me. This is Henry Leibowitz who will drive you home."

"How do you do?" said Henry.

"No, eaglet, no!" hollered Bridget.

"I'm not an eaglet, I'm a kosher chicken," I said. "And I can't write poetry either. I steal it. Also I lie practically every minute. Believe me, you couldn't have done worse."

"He's right, lady," said Henry.

"But try and remember that I did do one nice thing for you," I said. "I kept you from banning that schmuck Bruce Albright."

Then I gave her a little pat on the shoulder and went back to Celeste.

"Morris, I don't want you in my car," said Celeste.

"Shut up. I give the orders around here," I said.

"One more shut up and you're getting a hatpin in the eye," she said.

"Kiss me," I said.

"Like fun," she said.

So I grabbed her and we wrestled for a while but experience always tells in the end. In under five minutes I had her pinned and got my kiss and then naturally the you-know was on. It was the best one we ever had, a genuine axle-bender.

Celeste really appreciated it. "I'm glad you talked me into it, Morris," she said. "Frankly, Henry was terrible."

"Well, you won't be bothered with him any more," I said. "Or anybody else either, get me?"

"Oh, stop acting like a Jewish cave man," she said. "Tell me you love me. I want to hear how it sounds."

"I love you," I said.

"Still sounds like a whopper," she said.

"I don't give a damn how it sounds," I said. "You're gonna marry me and that's that."

"What if I don't?" she said.

"For openers I'll drive the car into the river," I said.

"Morris," she hollered, "do you know what the temperature is in the river?"

"Damn right," I said. "But I'll do it."

"No, you won't," said Celeste. "But it's the thought that counts. Okay, Morris, I guess you got a deal."

And that's how it happened, folks.

Chapter Twenty-one

Old A. M. Zimmerman kept scrapping right up to the end, I'll give him that. When Celeste told him we were going to get married, he right away called me over to his house, took me in the library, and showed me the codicil on his will. It was written by a goyish lawyer so it's pretty fancy language, but you'll get the idea. I quote:

"'In the devoutly hoped-against event that my daughter Celeste should perversely and in defiance of my strenuous wishes marry one Morris Katz, pauper, residing at 701 Selby Avenue, St. Paul, Minnesota, the said Celeste shall forfeit her share of my estate except for One Dollar only, and the balance shall be given to the B'nai Brith after sufficient funds have been set aside to commission a bust of myself in bronze for the lobbies of each of my 24 theatres.'"

"Well, I guess the wedding's off, right, Morris?" said Zimmerman.

"Wrong," I said. "And I'll tell you something else. You tried your best and you got nothing to be ashamed of. But you lost. So how's about being a good sport for a change?"

"No!" screamed Mrs. Zimmerman. "Fight on, Armand!"

But Zimmerman only gave a big sigh. "He's right,

Manya," he said to Mrs. Zimmerman. "I can't stop 'em from getting married no more. So there's only one thing to decide: shall I throw the both of 'em in the street, or shall I give 'em a wedding?"

"Here's my feeling," said Celeste. "Give us a wedding. If Morris works out, you'll change the codicil. If not, we'll *all* throw him in the street."

"That seems sensible," I said.

"But just a small wedding," said Celeste. "I don't want a vulgar spectacle like Morris's mother did."

"You'll have a vulgar spectacle and like it, God damn it!" hollered Zimmerman. "You think I'm gonna let that chicken-flicker Pearl Katz show me up?"

"Well, that's settled," I said. "Now let's talk about a date. Is next Sunday okay?"

Mrs. Zimmerman gave such a scream that half the crystals fell off the chandelier.

"Too soon?" I said. "All right, how's about a week from Sunday?"

"No, *two* weeks from Sunday," said Zimmerman. "That's Easter. Business will be horseshit anyways."

So that's when the wedding was set for. Then we cleared up some more details, like where would Celeste and me live (Celeste's room); did the Zimmermans want my folks to come over and discuss the wedding plans (shit, no); how many people Ma could invite from our side (only twelve and the men all had to wear a necktie); and then I went home to report the good news.

Well, naturally there was a terrific celebration. Everybody whooped and hollered including Nettie and Gittel who had no idea what was going on but they ran around and whacked their cymbals anyhow. But the best was Ma. I can't tell you how good it felt to see her acting like the old gut-shooter again—strutting around, lining people up, hollering orders, giving whammies.

"Libbie, stop crying on your dress," she said to my sister. "You got to wear it to the wedding."

"But, Mother, I thought my blue shantung," said Libbie.

"*I'm* wearing that," Ma said and turned to Jonathan. "Kaplan," she said, "I'll make you a deal. If you can keep from getting arrested till after the wedding, I'll call you Jonathan."

"You got it," said Jonathan.

"Nathan," said Ma to Pa, "don't forget to take your Dutch Boy sample book to the wedding. Maybe he needs a paint job, Zimmerman."

"Nettie and Gittel stole the book," said Pa.

"Look in the flue. That's where they're hiding everything," said Ma and then she turned to me. "Morris, my dolly, Morris, my sweet brilliant boychik," she said, "I got nothing to tell you. How could I tell you anything? Already you're smarter than your old mother."

"Oh, I don't know," I said.

"Shut up, I'm talking," Ma said. "So like I say, I got nothing to tell you. Just one little thing: between now and the wedding, every minute you ain't with Celeste you're gonna be with *me*, you hear?"

"I hear," I said.

"Nu, Kaplan, how's about a little peppiness?" said Ma. "It's a celebration or not?"

So Jonathan sang and danced and did some of his well-known imitations. I think the best one tonight was

Tarzan seeing a toilet for the first time, although Pius the XIth singing "Where Do You Worka, John" wasn't too far behind, believe me.

Later on Jonathan came up to me and gave me a big smile and a nice hug. "Morris," he said, "here's for you a mazeltov and my very, very best wishes."

"That's real nice of you," I said, "seeing as how you're the prick that thought I'd never pull it off."

"Well, kid, I'm glad I was wrong," he said. "Deeply and sincerely glad. All the same, a one-in-a-million fluke ain't exactly what you'd call a trend, and I certainly hope all your shlepper friends don't start in thinking, 'If Morris made it, why can't I?' Because there you got the curse of the world: people reaching longer than their arms. No, Morris, for your average shlepper I still say there's only one way to win: steal small."

And there you got the flaw in Jonathan's character— a wonderful guy, a big talent, a warm personality, but no vision. If only Jonathan had operated a little classier, how different his life would have been. And mine also, which you'll see in a minute.

Now I'll take you to Easter Sunday, 1937, and my wedding.

It was at the Nicollet Hotel in Minneapolis and I got to say it made Libbie's wedding look like a distress sale. Don't ask me who was there; ask me who *wasn't*. You couldn't spit in any direction without hitting at least a state senator. There must have been a thousand guests and every one was a Who's Who in Twin Cities Jewry except for the groom's side and naturally the goyim. And you remember Pflaum, that hoity-toity Reform rabbi who married Libbie? Well, Pflaum was there all right, but this time all he did was turn pages for the *main rabbi!*

I could go on for hours about how many pounds of strudel, how many gallons of seltzer, how many this, how many that, but I'll just tell you this one thing and if you're honest you'll admit you never saw anything like it at any wedding ever:

After the ceremony when Celeste and I left the chupah, we marched between two rows of one hundred ushers holding up crossed swords that Warner Brothers lent Zimmerman from *Captain Blood!* Now go equal that.

It was a sensational affair which they're still talking about in the Twin Cities and I enjoyed every second of it—until the catastrophe, that is. The catastrophe came just about an hour after the reception started in, and believe me it couldn't have happened at a moment of gayer merriment. The drinks and food were flowing, the guests were waltzing gracefully to the music of Si Silverman and His Society Strings—twenty-six men in maroon tuxes and a lady harpist in white—and everything looked so sparkling and hopeful that you couldn't even imagine a catastrophe was right on the doorstep.

But it was. All of a sudden a lady walked into the ballroom, about twenty-five years old, carrying a baby. The lady was a mess. Her hair was all straggly and she had on a brown sweater full of holes and her stockings were hanging. The baby was no collar ad either, if you want to know the truth.

So people turned and stared at her especially Zimmerman. What was this shabby person doing at such a stately function?

"You want something, missus?" said Zimmerman.

"I am looking for my husband Kirby Schwartz," said the lady.

"So go try the Salvation Army," said Zimmerman.

"I've come all the way from Cleveland," said the lady. "They told me I'd find him here."

"In *Cleveland* they told you?" said Zimmerman.

"No, in St. Paul," she said. "At the Katz residence on 701 Selby Avenue. The neighbors told me."

"What? What? What?" hollered Ma, running over.

"Oy, there he is!" screamed the lady, pointing out on the dance floor. "Here, hold Arnold," she said and gave Zimmerman the baby.

Then she went tearing out on the floor yelling, "Kirby! Kirby!" and heading straight for Jonathan Kaplan who was dancing with the governor's wife.

Jonathan gave one look at this lady running toward him and stopped dead. "Excuse me, Mrs. Stassen," he said to his partner and quicker than I can tell it, he turned around, ran out the door, ran down the steps four at a time, ran across the lobby, ran into Nicollet Avenue, and that's the last anybody ever saw of Jonathan Kaplan.

Or Kirby Schwartz, if that's his name. It took a long time to find out because first the lady from Cleveland went into hysterics, then Libbie, and then Ma. And of course, Mrs. Zimmerman too, but she *arrived* in hysterics.

But finally they got quietened down a little. A place was cleared for Mrs. Kirby Schwartz to sit down with Arnold, her baby, and everybody started in to gather around because naturally who wasn't interested? Mr. Zimmerman did the questioning.

"Why did you call that man Kirby Schwartz?" he said.

"That's what he told me his name was," said Mrs. Schwartz. "I don't know if it's right though because he got another name too."

"Jonathan Kaplan?" said Zimmerman.

"No, Winfield Feldman," said Mrs. Schwartz. "At least that's what the lady called him who came to my house a few months ago. She was from New York, and she had a baby also—a girl: Marilyn."

"And was she married to Kirby too?" said Zimmerman.

"Yes," said Mrs. Schwartz. "Only she called him Winfield Feldman like I said. He jumped out the window and ran away so I don't know who's right."

"And you're still married to Winfield?" said Zimmerman.

"To Kirby," she said. "Yes."

"So it looks like he got three wives anyhow," said Zimmerman. "One in St. Paul, one in Cleveland, and one in New York."

"And one before that," said Mrs. Schwartz. "From Hartford. She followed him to New York. Sherwood Goldenberg, she called him. She had a baby also. A girl, Ruthie, I think."

"Busy little fucker, ain't he?" said Zimmerman. "Well, Mrs. Schwartz, here's a dollar. You and Arnold go get something to eat. Celeste, come over here, I got to talk to you."

"Daddy, let's don't be hasty," said Celeste.

"Also let's don't waste time," said Zimmerman. "Celeste, we got two distinguished judges here by the wedding, Judge Tannenbaum and Judge Swanberg. Pick either one and we'll make an annulment one, two, three."

"We will, like fun," said Celeste. "What do I care about Morris's crooked in-laws? It's him I love."

"And I love her," I said.

This caused a lot of murmuring from the crowd, about half pro and half con. But there was no doubt where Zimmerman stood. "Celeste, this is your last chance," he said. "Are you gonna annul this cockaroach?"

"No," said Celeste. "Not yet anyhow."

"In that case, folks, this is still a wedding," said Zimmerman to the spectators. "Silverman, play music."

So the orchestra started again and the guests went back to dancing, and Zimmerman turned to Celeste. "Well, good-by, Celeste," he said. "We'll send your clothes to Morris's house. Good-by, you cockaroach. Come, Manya."

He picked up my mother-in-law off the floor and they walked out.

That was exactly six weeks ago, and here's how things stand today:

My wife Celeste and me are living with my folks on Selby Avenue. We've got Libbie's former room and Libbie, being single, sleeps on the davenport.

Libbie still cries a lot naturally, but she's a little more cheerful than she was because she finally had a date the other night. In fact, I arranged it. I thought of an eligible Jewish bachelor with a job and I brought him home for supper. Mr. Harwood, who else? What the hell, he sure isn't going to end up with the Homecoming Queen, not while his mother is alive.

Nettie and Gittel are still with us of course because where the hell am I going to find $200 to put them in the home? As for hocking some wedding presents to raise money, forget it. From A. M. Zimmerman there was naturally no present at all and from the rest of Celeste's fancy uptown relations all we got was pepper mills and nut-picks, which any pawnbroker will laugh right in your face. So at this moment the Nettie-Gittel situation is nothing to rave about.

Now here's one bright spot—two, actually. My cousin Crip is home from Rochester at last. And *cured,* isn't that marvelous! After all these years he can finally shake hands and ride in elevators and in fact, he even got laid last week for the first time and came through without so much as a hairline fracture. What happened was, now that Crip wasn't so brittle any more, he enrolled in the University. Naturally he wrote a few poems and he sent one of them to the *L'Etoile du Nord* and you guessed it: he met Bridget and pop went two cherries. I never saw a couple so crazy in love. Of course, it's heading nowheres. When Crip's mother finds out, he'll wish he was back in the cast. But I don't say anything to Crip. Let him enjoy while he can, the poor doomed fool.

And Albert? You'd think God would get bored, wouldn't you, torturing the same man all the time? Here's the latest: Albert came home from the Brainerd workhouse and naturally started looking for a job again. So one day an idea hit me: as long as somebody was going to get paid for fixing Sister Mary Frances's Angelus bell, why not Albert? True, he knew nothing about bells but so what? Wasn't he a mechanical genius? So I sent him to the convent, telling him not to mention my name naturally, and sure enough he got the job. So he went to work on the bell and by and by it looked to him like it was fixed. "Okay, give her a yank," he hollered down to Sister Mary Frances who was on the ground holding the rope. So she gave a yank. And Albert who as I said knows nothing about bells stood there with his head inside of it. Some of the doctors think it might clear up, but as of now he's stone deaf.

And that about wraps it up. If you're wondering about me, I'm not in such bad spirits, all things considered. I mean, a guy's got to keep up his hopes, otherwise you might as well jump off the Robert Street Bridge and be done with it. So I keep telling myself things are bound to get better. After all, Celeste is an only child. How long can that sonofabitch Zimmerman hold out? Sooner or later he got to start acting human. If nothing else softens him up, a grandchild certainly ought to do it. Not that Celeste is pregnant but it shouldn't be long. God knows we do enough humping.

And even if for some reason Celeste doesn't get pregnant, probably we can get a baby from that nympho Reba Jorgensen over on Dayton Avenue and say it's ours. Reba's about due again. Or maybe come winter my father will fall down and break his tailbone once more. Who knows what might happen? The point is, you're never a loser if you won't say you're licked.

Well, that's my story except for one last item. I saved

this one for the end because it kills me, it really does. Listen to this: the other night Celeste says to me, "Morris, do you still love me?"

"Of course," I say. "What a dumb question."

"So how come you don't write me any more poems?" she says.

Well, I almost die laughing, but the next day I'll be damned if I don't go to Crip and ask for a poem. Here it is:

TO CELESTE—AGAIN

I searched for a flower I'd never known,
I searched for a bloom I could not name,
I wandered the earth, beset, alone,
A ghostly player in a ghostly game.

Heartsick returned I to my room,
And there—praise God—'twas o'er, my quest!
There was the flower and there the bloom,
There in the garden called Celeste.

Both garden and woman? 'Tis too uncanny!
But, see, there blow the petals rife!
There nectar drips from every cranny!
Who else has such a blooming wife?

CWH